TALON

SHADOWRIDGE GUARDIANS MC, BOOK 6

PEPPER NORTH

PHOTOGRAPHY BY
ERIC D BATTLESHELL

COVER MODEL
ALEX PEREZ

Pepper North
With a Wink Publishing, LLC

ABOUT SHADOWRIDGE GUARDIANS MC

Combining the sizzling talents of bestselling authors Pepper North, Kate Oliver, and Becca Jameson, the Shadowridge Guardians are guaranteed to give you a thrill and leave you dreaming of your own throbbing motorcycle joyride.

Are you daring enough to ride with a club of rough, growly, commanding men? The protective Daddies of the Shadowridge Guardians Motorcycle Club will stop at nothing to ensure the safety and protection of everything that belongs to them: their Littles, their club, and their town. Throw in some sassy, naughty, mischievous women who won't hesitate to serve their fair share of attitude even in the face of looming danger, and this brand new MC Romance series is ready to ignite!

Shadowridge Guardians MC
Steele
Kade
Atlas
Doc
Gabriel

Talon
Bear
Faust
Storm

CHAPTER
ONE

"Horsefeathers!" Elizabeth cursed, losing her balance, and dropping her groceries. Strong hands steadied her, preventing her from tumbling to the ground along with the now bruised apples.

"Whoa. Are you okay?" a deep voice asked, making her look up at her rescuer.

For a split second too long, she stared at the young leather-clad biker standing in front of her, bringing a knowing smile to his face. "You could watch where you're going," she blustered, reacting aggressively due to embarrassment.

"I was actually just standing here," the magnetic biker pointed out. "You dashed through the door like you'd just robbed the place."

He paused for a moment before leaning closer to ask, "You didn't, did you?"

"Of course not!" Elizabeth answered, jerking herself out of his stabilizing hold. She squatted to pick up her scattered items, trying to move quickly.

"Let me help you," the tattooed gentleman offered.

Elizabeth's face flamed with heat when she automatically noticed the way his battered jeans molded to his thighs. She dragged her eyes away before she could check out everything. *I obviously need to get laid.*

"That's interesting. Are you propositioning me?" the man asked with merriment dancing in his gaze.

"Oh, holy duck. I didn't mean to say that out loud. Sorry. Just hand me that orange and I'll go hide," she demanded.

"Has anyone ever told you you're not very good at cussing?" he asked as he nabbed the last escapee and held it out to her.

Rolling her eyes, Elizabeth snatched the orange and stuffed it back in her bag. "Only my obnoxious husband and I just got rid of him," she reported as she stood and adjusted her slim skirt back down her thighs.

She pulled herself together and forced herself to be polite. "Thank you for your help. I'm sorry I plowed into you."

"I'm not," he answered with a smile. Holding out his hand, he added, "I'm Talon."

"Of course, you are. And I'm way too old for you."

"I don't think that's your name," he said. His voice held a new tone.

Commanding and dominant, it captured her attention, making her stop and fully look at him for the first time. Elizabeth swallowed hard at the steel in his gaze.

"Elizabeth," she admitted.

"That suits you. I'm glad to meet you, Elizabeth." He still held out his hand.

She stared at it for a second. Something inside told her touching him would change everything. When he didn't draw his back, Elizabeth slowly placed her hand in his. Warmth, strength, and something she didn't understand registered deep inside her. In surprise, she looked up at him, meeting his dark eyes.

"I didn't expect to meet you today, Little girl," he said softly.

Snatching her hand from his, she ran toward her car. Her heart pounded inside her chest, and she didn't even want to think about why her panties were damp.

Fluffernutter! What just happened?

"Talon, saddle up. We need to go," a gruff voice called as she fumbled with the door handle of her car.

She looked back at the magnetic man who'd just rocked her world with one touch. He stood watching her. His entire attention was focused on her. Shivering in reaction, Elizabeth jumped into her car and thrust the grocery sack into the passenger seat. The already bruised fruit bounced to the floorboard.

Starting the car, she risked one last glance. Talon had moved. Elizabeth scanned the area and spotted him just as he lifted a leg over his massive bike. She bit her lip and made herself focus on the parking lot as she backed out and drove away, hearing the roar of powerful motors firing to life behind her.

"Don't let them be going my way. Don't let them be going my way. Don't let them be going my way," she chanted as she turned to the left.

Elizabeth divided her attention between the road in front and behind her. To her relief, the powerful throb of the motors faded into the background. They'd turned to the right.

Slumping in her seat, she drove away, making herself focus on the road as she navigated her way toward her new apartment. Her lawyer had assured her she would be awarded the house if she chose to ask for it. A flash of her ex in bed with the floozy next door appeared in her head.

"Nope. I couldn't ever stay in that house again," she announced to the tattered bag of groceries. The oranges seemed to understand where she was coming from at least while the apples just pouted at the treatment they'd experienced.

A memory of the thin woman who didn't even attempt to cover her nakedness flashed into her head, making Elizabeth instantly sick—mentally and physically. To distract herself, Elizabeth joked, "Come on. She would have juiced you apples for sure." They still did not choose to respond.

"This is my life now. Holding a conversation with fruit."

Flipping on the radio, Elizabeth distracted herself with the local news report. There were so many people out there dealing with much greater problems than she had. Shaking her head, she told herself to get over it. Thank goodness she hadn't wasted another ten years on that jerk.

An image of the biker popped into her mind. She'd never gone for the bad boy type. It must be just a reaction to the divorce. After her husband's betrayal, her mind was running from the chubby and reliable office type that hadn't worked out too well for her to one that instantly made her think of hot sex. Who would have known she was attracted to leather and smirks?

Feathers! She bet he knew exactly what he was doing in the bedroom. Maybe even over the kitchen counter or on the table. If people outside of books really did that.

It was Friday afternoon and a long weekend stretched in front of her. Throwing herself into work had distracted and occupied her attention. Now, she would have way too much time to think.

With a sigh, Elizabeth pulled into a parking spot and gathered her groceries one more time. She pulled the edges of the torn paper sack together to prevent another catastrophe and bumped her car door closed with her hip. Walking up to the second floor, Elizabeth unlocked her front door and headed for the kitchen.

It took exactly six minutes to put away the food—and then only that long because she'd washed the bruised produce before hiding them in a drawer in the almost empty refrigerator. She glanced at the healthy contents she'd purchased and sighed. What she really wanted was something dripping with calories.

Grabbing her phone to order a pizza with the works, she noticed a message from Janine. One of the younger women at the office, Janine had reached out a friendly hand when she'd read about Elizabeth's divorce in the paper. It turned out she was watching for hers to be announced.

> Hey. No moping at home. You're coming to The Hangout with me. I'll pick you up at seven.

Quickly, Elizabeth texted back.

> Go on without me. I'm going to order pizza and watch a movie.

> Too late. I'm at your door.

Three knocks landed on her door, making her jump. Rolling her eyes for the second time that night, Elizabeth went to answer and give her excuses.

What am I going to tell her? That I have an appointment with my vibrator?

"Hi, Janine. I'm sorry I didn't see your message sooner. I would have kept you from coming my way."

"I'm not taking no for an answer. I want the Hangout's trashcan nachos and I can't order them by myself. Take pity on me."

An image of the caloric treat of crisp tortilla chips with cheese sauce and salsa as well as sausage and jalapenos made her mouth water. "That sounds really good," Elizabeth confessed. "I was going to order pizza, but..." Her stomach was already growling at the thought of nachos.

"Pizza's great, but nothing beats those nachos. Come on. Put on some jeans and some dancing shoes. You and I are going to have some fun tonight," Janine ordered.

"All right, but I'll follow you in case I want to come home earlier than you," Elizabeth stated firmly.

"Nope. I'll drink too much if I'm just driving myself. With you there, I'll limit myself to one Bahama Mama and then I'll drink soft drinks the rest of the night."

"You'll bring me home when I want to come home?" Elizabeth pressed.

"Promise." Janine crossed her fingers over her heart.

"Fine. But I'm not dancing."

"Oh, you're dancing. If it makes you feel less nervous, I'm going to make you look good." Janine demonstrated some of her dance moves, making Elizabeth laugh.

"Fiddlesticks, we both suck at dancing?" Elizabeth threw over her shoulder as she walked into her bedroom to change.

"You are absolutely the worst at cussing! Fiddlesticks!" Janine said, laughing as she settled on the couch in the main room.

"I know. It's okay." Elizabeth laughed at herself. Her parents had been very strict about using foul language. They didn't use it at all so despite all her friends turning the air blue with their cussing, Elizabeth couldn't even think of anything to say when an occasion arose.

She discarded her office clothes and jumped into some jeans. Elizabeth couldn't help noticing they fit looser than before. Planning ahead, she added a tank top and sandals. It would be packed in there on a Friday night. Elizabeth might as well walk in looking cool.

CHAPTER
TWO

"Who was that?" Faust asked when they pulled up to their reserved parking area in the back of The Hangout.

Talon looked at the tall, bald biker as he took off his helmet and brushed a hand through his hair. "That was my Little girl."

"Right," Faust scoffed.

"Really. She's mine. Her name is Elizabeth."

"Does Elizabeth have a clue you even exist?"

"Oh, yeah. She knows I exist," Talon answered confidently as he stood up and swung a leg over the powerful bike. He'd seen the awareness in her eyes that something special had happened.

Shrugging, Faust looked skeptical. "Whatever. Let's go join the others. Hopefully someone will spark a brawl tonight. I feel like getting my muscles warmed up," Faust stated in a flat voice.

"Just like a normal Friday night for you, huh? You know you don't have to be a royal ass to everyone. I think you're a nice guy on the inside."

Faust's cussing made everyone look. Talon laughed, totally not put off by the big man's flash of anger. He leaned into whisper, "I won't tell anyone."

Faust shook his head. "You live in the land of delusions."

"You know you love me," Talon teased, poking at his Shadowridge Guardians brother.

Faust swung his leg over his bike and suggested, "Let's go in before I take the pretty off your face."

Laughing, Talon joined him as Faust headed toward the bar doors. "You lead. Everyone automatically gets out of your way."

Usually, the president of the MC would lead the guys into battle, but the most dangerous thing about The Hangout was the disco music the DJ insisted on sneaking in between the more current hits. Talon didn't care. He automatically moved to the beat, enjoying the rhythm.

A roar went up as Faust walked in with a fierce scowl on his face. The club always started the party in the bar. The MC didn't end up there every night, but when they rolled in, the energy level doubled. Girls attracted by bad boys streamed in, and guys eager to console those that didn't catch one of the biker's eyes followed, hoping for a chance.

Talon was well known as a dancing machine. Free of any commitments, his lack of an old lady made him a popular choice for women who wanted a taste of life on the wild side. Usually, he welcomed all the attention. Tonight, it didn't seem right to flirt with random women. He grabbed a beer from the waitress and leaned against the wall, talking to other club members.

"Watch this," he said to Doc as a woman approached Faust just as the DJ played a slow song.

The two men focused on the statuesque brunette who approached the scowling biker. She almost shook in front of him, nervous to dare ask the man with a well-known temper to dance. Faust simply let her talk.

"This isn't going to end well," Doc commented.

To their amazement, Faust pushed away from the wall after a second's pause and took the young woman's hand. He led her to the dance floor as the woman looked behind her in shock and triumph at her friends who hooted and hollered to encourage her. Seconds later, wrapped in his arms, the woman closed her eyes as she rested against Faust's powerful body.

"Damn! There goes another one. Who would have imagined the devil himself would be the catch of the night?" Talon joked.

Scanning the bar, he saw the back of a woman's head and started forward without listening to Doc's response. *It couldn't be.* He watched that familiar figure take a seat at a table with another woman. They caught the waitress as she walked by. As the server walked away to put in an order, Talon met her gaze and patted himself on the chest.

"On your tab?" the familiar employee asked as she passed Talon.

"Yes."

"You got it. I'll let them know."

"That won't be necessary," Talon assured her.

"Good luck!" With a smile, the server sashayed through the crowd.

Continuing through the crowd, Talon circled to the front of the table to greet the ladies. "Good evening," he said to both before focusing on Elizabeth. "I'm glad to run into you again."

"You know Talon?" Janine said with a shocked look.

"You know his name?" Elizabeth asked her friend, trying not to focus on the man before her.

"Of course. Everyone knows Talon," Janine informed her before holding her hand out to greet him. "Hi, I'm Janine."

"Hi, Janine. Is it you I should thank for bringing Elizabeth here tonight?" he asked knowingly.

"I bribed her with nachos," Janine confirmed.

"Hey. I'm right here," Elizabeth said assertively, looking uncomfortable at being left out of the conversation focused on her.

"I know. And I'm thanking the woman who dragged you here," Talon said before giving Elizabeth a slow smile.

"Janine, do you mind if I steal Elizabeth?" he asked.

"Not at all," her friend said with a laugh and a shooing gesture.

Before she knew what was happening, he had gallantly helped her out of her chair. Three steps away from the table, Elizabeth hesitated. "I don't want to leave her alone."

"Oh, she won't be alone," Talon assured her and turned to meet the gaze of one of the pledges hanging on the outskirts of the bar. He nodded at Janine and the muscular man immediately made his way through the crowd with a big smile on his face.

"I don't know how to dance." Elizabeth threw the warning out there as they stepped onto the dance floor.

"I do. Leading is my job. Just follow me and have fun," Talon reassured her, drawing her close to his body. Talon might look rough now, but his parents were world-class Latin dancers. He'd grown up in a house set up for dancing at a moment's notice. He definitely couldn't cook without the radio on to fuel a boogie across the floor as he chopped or stirred.

He taught her a simple dance of a few steps and kept it easy until she began to move into it. "Keep the same steps," he directed before encouraging her, "Let's have some fun."

Talon easily moved her into a turn and saw the smile on her face widen to a grin. *She's perfect.* His Little girl liked to dance. Celebrating, Talon turned himself, leading her around his body, and heard her gasp in excitement. The move looked fancy, but it was the same footwork, just in a different direction. He alternated the different patterns, creating something unique and entertaining.

"This is so fun!" she shouted over the crowd and the music.

"You're doing great," he said, grinning at her. "And you told me you didn't dance."

When the music slowed once again, Talon pulled her close to sway to the beat. Putting his lips next to her ear, he whispered, "You know what happens to Little girls who lie, don't you?"

She froze in his arms and jolted a step away to stare at him with equal parts fascination and shock. "What happens?" she asked.

"Come here."

He pulled her back into his arms and held her until she softened against him once again. Only then did he whisper, "Their Daddies punish them, of course. That's what happens to bad Little girls."

"Stop playing with me," she hissed.

"No way, Little girl. You're the one I've dreamed of playing with. I'm afraid you're stuck with me. Some nachos are on the way to your table. Shall we take a break so you can eat a very unnutritious dinner?"

"Treats are good for your soul," she said loftily, turning to walk off the dance floor and leaving him there.

He weaved his fingers with hers as he caught up with her. When she looked back at him, Talon moved ahead to make a path through the dancers as they weaved their way toward her table.

"Thanks. It was packed out there," she said when they reached the edge of the dance floor.

"I hope you'll always think it's nice to have me around," Talon commented lightly as he squeezed her hand. "And I agree, treats *are* good for your soul."

At the table, he helped Elizabeth onto her tall bar chair with an ease that was designed to erase any awkwardness. She smiled her appreciation. Talon skillfully maneuvered his chair a bit closer and took a seat next to her. Janine was flushed and leaning close to the large, tattooed man next to her.

"Elizabeth, this is Ink. He's a prospect for the club. Ink, this is Elizabeth. She's mine," Talon said easily.

"Yours? Wait a minute," Elizabeth protested, looking flustered.

"Got it, Talon," Ink acknowledged Talon's claim without question.

The arrival of the server with the nachos cut off any further comment from Elizabeth. With a flourish, the waitress placed the tray on top of the small, metal trashcan and flipped it over. Lifting the can up, the contents tumbled over the tray. The smell was delectable.

"Need any drinks?" she asked and left with an order from everyone.

Janine waved her hand over the tray and encouraged everyone, "Dig in. There is way too much for even four of us to eat."

Elizabeth picked up a chip, and scooped up some of the goodies. He noticed she cautiously avoided a huge slice of jalapeno. Talon followed behind her and swooped in to help himself to that ring of fire.

"You can eat those?" Elizabeth asked.

"Oh, yeah. I do avoid them if I plan on certain activities," Talon shared.

Elizabeth looked at him in confusion as she tried to figure out what he was talking about. She looked over at Janine. Her friend shook her head, like she knew but wasn't going to say. *When would he need to avoid eating jalapenos if they didn't affect him too much?*

Deciding not to worry about it, Elizabeth took another bite. Changing the subject, she asked Ink, "How long is someone a prospect for a motorcycle club?"

"That's up to the members. I just keep showing up and hope they'll decide they need me," Ink shared.

"There are a lot of MCs out there. Some people are perfect for one and totally not for others. Ink fits in well. He's right that showing his commitment to the club is important," Talon said. "Well, that and not pissing someone off."

Ink shook his head and laughed. There was obviously a story there that they shared.

"So, you all like sell drugs and drag people who try to stop you behind your motorcycles?" she asked breezily.

Instantly, Ink stiffened and even Janine sat straight in shock. Talon, on the other hand, just laughed it off.

"You've been watching too much TV. The Shadowridge Guardians are a motorcycle club not a gang. We help the community and do good works," Talon told her.

"Really? You don't beat people up and claim a territory?" Elizabeth asked lightheartedly. She didn't know why she was poking the bear, but she couldn't help herself.

"Oh, yeah, we do that, if necessary," Talon acknowledged.

"Hmm," Elizabeth commented.

Janine hissed, "What has gotten into you? I'm sorry, Elizabeth isn't a judgmental soul. Her divorce has twisted her into a negative mindset. It's easy to do. I'm in the process as well."

Talon proposed a toast, raising his beer bottle to clink against Ink's. "To the assholes who didn't realize how lucky they were."

Janine immediately raised the last of her Bahama Mama to join them. Elizabeth sat quietly, subdued for the first time that evening. She hated to admit that her soon-to-be ex's accusations of how she had forced him to have an affair with someone else had wormed their way into her brain. Maybe it was her fault.

Talon's warm hand covered hers and she looked up in surprise. "Stop thinking so hard. No man is worth that."

"Sorry."

"No sorries. Eat, Buttercup. You're hungry, and I plan to dance your shoes off."

Nodding, she loaded another chip with all the good stuff and popped it into her mouth. As she bit down, her eyes watered. A hidden jalapeno had disguised itself under a dollop of sour cream. Trying to be brave, she chewed, feeling the fire building with each chomp.

"Spit it out," Talon commanded and placed a few napkins at

her mouth. He nodded when she looked at him to double-check. "Get rid of it. It's going to get hotter."

For self-preservation, she followed his instruction and pushed the bite out of her mouth. Talon wrapped it up without a grimace or reaction and handed Elizabeth her frozen drink. Grateful, she took a large gulp and then another.

As she extinguished the fire in her mouth, Talon carefully picked through the stack of nachos in front of her to pull out a dozen honker jalapeno slices. He set them in front of him and loaded another bite with all the goodies and no peppers.

"Try this one," he said, lifting it to her lips.

Automatically, she opened her mouth and let him feed her. The cool sour cream helped soothe her still burning tongue and Elizabeth smiled at him. Raising one hand, she covered her mouth and thanked him.

"No talking with your mouth full, Buttercup," he admonished before starting a new line of conversation with Janine and Ink.

"Do you both work together, Janine?"

"We do. Not in the same department, but our roles overlap from time to time," the other woman answered. "We've gone out a few times. Well, I've forced Elizabeth to come out with me."

"Good. I'm glad." Talon smiled his approval.

Feeling slightly jealous, Elizabeth was amazed when she found herself scooting closer to Talon as if staking her claim. She started to move back over, but Talon wrapped a hand around her thigh and squeezed to hold her in place. The server brought their new drinks over and Elizabeth noticed that Janine had switched to a soft drink. She took another drink of her frozen concoction and knew she should do that, too. Elizabeth didn't want to lose her common sense around Talon. She could handle this one though. It was so good.

"What do you do, Ink?" Janine asked.

"I'm a surgeon," he joked. "No, I'm a tattoo artist. That's how

I connected with the Shadowridge Guardians. I've done some work on several members."

"I've been thinking about getting a rose on my ankle," Janine said, holding a foot out under the table to show the spot she was considering for the artwork.

"When you're ready, come talk to me. There are some things I always recommend people think about before putting something into their bodies," Ink said.

Elizabeth smiled to herself. It seemed like Ink was a stand-up guy. She was glad Janine had met someone nice.

"Recovered?" Talon asked.

She shook her head ruefully. "Almost. That was awful. Sorry to be a wimp."

"You haven't seen me on sushi night," Talon said with a laugh.

"Wasabi?"

"I'm not eating raw fish for anyone. They tricked me into it once. That will be the last time," Talon vowed.

Ink, overhearing, tried to control his belly-deep laughter. Talon pointed at him and warned, "Don't forget what happened to Gabriel. There's no telling what pay back I might devise for you."

"I don't think anyone is going to ever get that out of their memory," Ink said, dissolving into guffaws that made everyone, including Talon, laugh.

"What did you do?" Elizabeth asked, wide-eyed.

"Talon painted his bedroom black. It looked great until Gabriel went to sleep. Then, all these rainbow-colored fluorescent specks showed up. Gabriel thought it felt like he was in a freaking underwater aquarium," Ink shared. "His... His girlfriend loved it."

Why did it sound like he covered up something else he started to say?

Pushing that thought out of her mind, Elizabeth imagined

sparkling walls that made the night less scary. "That sounds amazing. I would have loved to see that."

"I don't think he got a lot of sleep until he repainted it," Talon confessed. "It took six coats of paint to extinguish the glow."

"No way," Janine said with a hoot of laughter.

"What can I say? I leave an impact," Talon suggested modestly.

Conversation lulled for a bit as a rocking loud song made it hard to hear well. Elizabeth found herself chuckling at random moments at Talon's antics. He leaned close to whisper into her ear.

"What's so funny, Little girl?"

"That room thing. You're so bad," she said, giggling.

"Or so good," he suggested as he kissed her temple. "Ready to dance some more?"

Throwing caution to the wind, she answered with her heart. "Please."

CHAPTER
THREE

Waking up in her own bed the next morning, Elizabeth wrapped her arms around herself and just remembered. It seemed like such a magical night—dancing with Talon, laughing way too much, and having the time of her life. She'd hated for the night to end.

The guys had walked them out to Janine's car. Elizabeth had never felt safer in her life. When one guy had cat-called them, Talon's look of death had made her shiver, and the jokester waved his apologies before walking away.

Could she date a biker? Her mother would be completely against it. Elizabeth imagined taking him home for the holiday meal. That would be a conversation starter.

She grinned at the thought of Talon charming them all. He was such a smart ass, but that covered a great guy underneath. Or, at least, she thought it did.

Don't fall too head over heels.

Pulling her stuffed dragon toward her, Elizabeth buried her face in his green fur to give Puff a kiss before leaning him back slightly. "You know he thinks I'm his Little girl."

Pausing to listen for a few seconds, she answered Puff's response. "I don't know how he knows. He's pretty confident."

After his next question, she was forced to admit, "I like him a lot."

When Puff ran out of questions, Elizabeth checked the time. The weekend farmer's market would be open. She might as well go pick up some fresh produce. The tomatoes there were always the best.

Rolling out of bed, she quickly pulled the covers into place with Puff snuggled between the pillows in his favorite spot. After using the toilet, she washed her face and hands. Pausing to look at her reflection, she grinned at her bare face and shrugged. Elizabeth hated wearing makeup. It was great on the weekend to have free time to just be her and not the business professional Elizabeth who she had carefully cultivated.

She pulled on a pair of shorts and a casual top before picking up the basket she always carried to the market. This way, she didn't have any plastic bags to take to the recycle place. Elizabeth wasn't uber green, but she did try to do easy things to help the environment.

The grounds were packed with people. Everyone was in a good mood, enjoying the beautiful weather and the weekend. Elizabeth snagged a few tomatoes and cucumbers, planning to make a Greek salad she could take to work next week. She stopped to look at some baby onions that wouldn't be too strong.

A loud voice drew her attention away from the display. Looking up, she followed the sound with her gaze to see a rough looking man in a leather biker's vest, standing over a female vendor. She couldn't hear his words distinctly, but the tone was harsh and berating.

Surely the Shadowridge Guardians didn't treat people like this. The crowd edged away, creating an empty space. Pissed, Elizabeth didn't think of her own safety. If no one was going to step in, she'd do it. Elizabeth worked her way through the ring of spectators to the woman's side.

"Hey. I don't know what's going on, but you don't talk to anyone like this!" she said calmly, interrupting the man's tirade.

"Get the hell out of here, do-gooder."

"Do you see how many people are filming you?" Elizabeth pointed out, wrapping an arm around the trembling target's waist to give her some support.

"I don't care if I end up on the evening news. This bitch just needs to cough up what I need, and I'll be on my way."

"I don't have any more honey. This isn't the time to harvest, and you stole my supply from last fall two weeks ago." The frightened woman tried to stand up for herself.

"I don't believe that. I'll just look for myself." Sneering, he circled the table to enter the area where the vendor had stashed her extra items.

Picking up a jar of pickled beets, he tossed it over his shoulder, barely missing an onlooker and shattering the jar on the hard, trampled ground. Those close by jumped back to avoid the splash of red juice.

"Get out of here," Elizabeth shouted. "She doesn't have any honey! And you stole the last supply."

Looking around at the crowd, she demanded, "Someone call the police!" Elizabeth knew better than to take her gaze off the jerk in front of her.

Holding her basket in front of her as a shield, Elizabeth stepped in front of the other woman, protecting her. Elizabeth knew she had to look ridiculous. All one hundred and twenty pounds of her, standing on her tiptoes to make herself look taller in front of an angry man who had to weigh two fifty.

"I'll be out of here with everything I want before the police can get here," the brute scoffed at her as he stepped menacingly closer.

"Hey, Buttercup. Did you find those pastries the guys wanted?" a familiar voice called from the side of the standoff.

Surprised, Elizabeth turned to see Talon and five large bikers approaching from the crowd which divided readily to allow them through. Torn between being happy to see his handsome face and concerned that the situation had just become worse, she tightened her fingers around the handle of her basket.

"Your biker buddy is trying to shake down this woman," she answered, focusing back on the threat.

"He's not a Shadowridge Guardian," a tall, built man with short hair assured her. "We wouldn't take him. Seems like we made a good decision."

"Fuck you, Steele. Like I ever wanted to be part of your pansy group."

"Sure. Let's go with that. You need to back off. Twenty people already called the police. They'll be here in two minutes," Steele said firmly as Talon kept approaching.

"Hey, Buttercup," Talon greeted her and pressed a kiss to her temple before lifting Elizabeth off her feet to place her behind him.

"Want to pick on someone your own size?" Talon asked the hulking man in front of him.

The man scoffed and sized up Talon. "I've got a good sixty pounds on you."

"Yeah, but yours is all padding and mine is ready to kick your butt," Talon answered.

Looking at the back of his head, Elizabeth could hear the shit-eating grin that had to accompany his assertion. She wanted to tell him to be safe but didn't want to distract him.

The sound of distant sirens caught her attention. The noise increased as the two stood squared off against each other. Elizabeth could feel the tension radiating from Talon's body while he stood nonchalantly. She was amazed he seemed totally unfazed by the bully in front of him.

"Oh, yeah. With your friends behind you to back you up, you're tough. I'll just be the bigger guy and walk away now," the other biker sneered.

"Stellar idea," Talon congratulated him.

With a snort of disgust, the man turned and created a path

through the gathered crowd. Talon watched until he was completely out of sight before turning.

"You live an exciting life, Little girl," he commented.

"Thanks for coming." She slipped her hand into Talon's and squeezed his. Even with a million unpleasant work experiences, Elizabeth didn't like confrontations. She could feel herself shaking and tried to get it under control.

"I'm glad the Chaplain wanted some corn to grill for dinner. How did you get involved in this?" he asked.

Talon pulled her closer to wrap his arms around her. Resting her head against his chest, Elizabeth allowed herself to absorb some of his strength. In the distance, she heard the sound of a rough motorcycle engine sputtering to life.

Steele commented to the other members around him, "Glad he won't be bringing that trash for us to fix."

Hoping Talon would forget his question, Elizabeth rotated in his arms to look at the vendor to ask, "Are you okay?"

"I am. Thanks to you, I still have some things to sell. Looks like I need to talk to the people who organize the market to urge them to get some security in here," the woman said as she straightened her shoulders. "I should get that broken glass picked up. I don't want anyone to get cut."

"I think the guys have it," Talon assured her and lifted a hand from Elizabeth's back to wave at the group of bikers who'd stationed themselves around the glass as Steele picked up the shards.

"Thank you all," the woman called. "And thank you, miss. You jumped into a bad situation. Not the smartest thing to do, but I appreciate your support."

"It was nothing," Elizabeth said, glancing sideways at Talon who had stiffened next to her, his arms tightening around her.

The woman nodded and smiled. "Can I send you home with a can of my market-famous beets? Just as a special thank you?"

"I'd love that. Thank you." Elizabeth stepped away from the

security of Talon's arms to accept the beets. She missed his support immediately.

"Here. You take one, too." The vendor thrust one at Talon.

"Thank you, ma'am. I hope the rest of your day is amazing. Everyone should support you," Talon said, the last sentence at a louder volume. Instantly, she had a crowd at her booth.

He eased Elizabeth away as the woman turned to help her customers. Placing his jar in Elizabeth's basket, he plucked the handles from her hands and held it out for her to stow hers as well. Before they moved away from the booth, he tucked a twenty into the case containing the beets.

"Thanks. I'll pay you back," Elizabeth whispered.

"Not going to happen, Little girl. Come meet everyone," he requested as he wrapped an arm around her waist. Not waiting for her response, he guided her a few steps away from the booth to the rough-looking, disturbingly handsome men in leather.

"Elizabeth, these are my brothers. Steele, Doc, Gabriel, Kade, and Rock."

"Thanks for showing up at the right time," she said quickly, noting the bikers each looked at how Talon held her close to his side. "Who was that guy?"

"That asshole calls himself Vengeance. His real name is Marion," Gabriel answered her before looking at Steele for guidance on how much to tell her.

"We're glad we were here," Steele assured her. "We'll go look for some corn. Bring Elizabeth to dinner, Talon."

"Oh, I couldn't..."

"We'll be there," Talon assured him.

He waited for the others to walk away before saying to Elizabeth, "If you ever put yourself in danger again, I'm going to spank your bottom until you can't sit down for days."

"What? You can't threaten me like that," she blustered while at the same time heat flared low in her belly.

"That is not a threat, Buttercup," he said, drawing her away from the crowd and to a secluded spot under a large oak tree.

Backing her up against the wide trunk, he set the basket down and leaned his hands on either side of her shoulders to pin her in place. "You scared me, Little girl."

He leaned in to kiss her hard before moving closer and tugging her to his body. With his arms wrapped around her, Talon captured her lips once again. When he lifted his head, she could only stare at him with passion-glazed eyes.

After a few seconds, she whispered, "I'm sorry."

"Never again, Little girl. Call the police, go get someone in authority, hell, gather a crowd, but don't ever stand up to a bully by yourself. We'll take care of the Devil's Jesters. Okay?"

"Okay. Can I have another kiss?" she blurted, unable to believe he had rocked her world so much.

This time, Talon changed his tactics. His mouth met hers in a tender kiss that made her knees weak. She responded to it eagerly as she tangled her hands in his thick black hair. This time when he raised his head, she blurted, "You wouldn't really spank me, right?"

"Wrong. This was your only warning." His look told her he wasn't joking. "Let me have your phone."

Elizabeth pulled it out of her back pocket and handed it over. She watched Talon put his number into her phone. He'd handed her a napkin with his number on it last night, but she hadn't stopped this morning to type it in. She watched him ring his number and check on his own phone that he had her number before handing it back.

Talon lifted a hand to cradle her chin. "Call me if you're in a pinch. Even if I can't convince you that I'm your Daddy, I'll come as fast as possible to help—as will the rest of the Shadowridge Guardians. I've claimed you now."

"Really?" she squeaked. "I mean, we just danced a bit last night."

"We danced our asses off, Buttercup. Had there been a dance award, we would have won!" Talon crowed, making her laugh and dispelling the last of the tension.

"Did you finish your shopping?" he asked.

"I wanted to get some baby onions for my Greek salad."

"Let's go finish up. Have you had breakfast?"

"No. But it's almost lunch time," she pointed out with a laugh.

"Lunch it is," he announced.

"You don't have to take me to lunch."

"I don't, but I want to. You're coming to dinner at the clubhouse. We might as well spend the day together. That is, unless you have other plans?"

"I don't have anything particular on my schedule. Are you sure they want me at the dinner tonight?" she asked as Talon picked up her basket and slung it over his muscular forearm.

Taking her hand, Talon squeezed it. "The president of the MC asked you himself. You *have* to come now."

"Really?" she squeaked for the second time in just a few minutes.

"Really." As they merged into the crowd, many people smiled at them. Elizabeth returned the friendly greeting as she turned her attention to the perfect onions. "That was the booth I was going to visit when all the ruckus started."

"Let's go."

A few minutes later, she had exactly what she'd hoped to find. Talon paid for her choice despite her protests and made an extra stop at a vendor with flowers. The colorful bouquet he chose was gorgeous, and Elizabeth had to keep herself from dancing at his side from pure happiness as they walked back to the parking lot. She couldn't remember the last time someone had given her flowers.

"Let's take these back to your house, Buttercup. Where's your car?"

"My apartment is about a fifteen-minute walk from here. I just came by foot," she admitted.

"Perfect. We'll drop off the veggies and put your flowers in water before heading to lunch. We'll have burgers tonight. What do you think of seafood?"

"It's good when it's cooked?" she suggested with a grin, referring to the sushi incident.

"Amen. Let's go."

When they reached his huge bike, she couldn't help thinking that the owner and his motorcycle were a perfect match. The power and sexy styling of the machine complimented the sensual vibes that radiated from Talon. When he opened one of his saddlebags and pulled out a fuzzy pink bear, she reached automatically to cuddle the stuffie against her chest.

"He's so cute," she whispered.

"Poor guy's been tired of hanging with me. I thought you might like him," Talon said. His tone was light, but she sensed this was important.

"Thank you. I love him." Elizabeth hugged the teddy bear again and kissed the top of his head. "I think I'll name him Borscht."

"After the cold beet soup?" Talon asked. His black eyes danced with amusement.

"Yes. It seems appropriate for a dashing, pink teddy bear of the male persuasion."

"How did you know Borscht was a boy?" Talon asked, raising his eyebrow.

"Come on. It's so obvious," she teased, squeezing the bear close once again and rubbing her chin over his furry head.

She shouldn't love this bear so much. But she did. Elizabeth crossed her fingers, hoping Borscht and Puff would become besties.

"How about if Borscht rides in your basket?" Talon asked.

"He won't fall out?"

"I'll make sure he's okay," Talon promised.

"Okay."

Within a few minutes, he had her basket bungeed securely on his rear carrier with Borscht tucked safely inside. Talon pulled an extra helmet from the other saddlebag on his bike. Carefully, he fit it on her head and brushed the strands of hair that fluttered around her face away as he tightened the chin strap. "That's a bit too big, but it will keep you safe until we get one your size."

"That won't be necessary. I won't need it. You are a safe driver, right?"

"I am."

"Whew. Okay. Can I just shout directions?"

"How about you tell me now?"

She recited the route to her apartment. There were several turns and Elizabeth double checked when she was finished. "Does that make sense?"

"Got it. Now, have you ever ridden on a bike?"

"When I was a kid, my uncle took me on a few rides. I just lean when you do, right?"

"That's it. Keep your feet on the pegs," he directed, leaning down to flip them away from their stowed position flush against the bike. "The pipes are hot. I don't want you to get burned."

"Okay. I'll be careful."

"Alright, let's go." In a move that screamed athleticism, he swung a leg over the huge motorcycle and gestured for her to join him.

Trying to be at least half as graceful as him, Elizabeth scrambled over the bike that was much taller than her legs. With his arm boosting her, she finally slid onto the seat.

"Feet on the pegs and arms around my waist," he reminded her after starting the throbbing engine.

Trying to keep her distance from him, she placed her hands on his waist. Talon wrapped an arm around behind her and pulled her firmly against him before tugging her hands together in front of his hard stomach. Elizabeth closed her eyes to savor the feel of being wrapped around his muscular body.

"Better. Now, the foot pegs," he reminded her, and Elizabeth scrambled to lift her feet from the ground and into place. "Let's ride."

CHAPTER
FOUR

Talon pulled out of the parking space smoothly and emerged from the lot with an ease that demonstrated how much experience he had in controlling a bike. After the first corner, Elizabeth relaxed against him and earned a squeeze of her thigh with his powerful hand. She smiled against his back, pleased by his approval.

Elizabeth was sorry when he pulled into her apartment complex and backed the bike into a parking space. She didn't want to admit even to herself how much she enjoyed having an excuse to snuggle close to his powerful body.

"Here you are. All in one piece," he announced, cutting through her thoughts.

"You're good," she complimented, scrambling off and standing back to watch him. Elizabeth wished she was as graceful as he was in easing off the monster bike.

"I know. But I'm glad you noticed. Let's take this up to your apartment and we can go have lunch," Talon suggested as he unfastened her basket.

"Want to take my car?" she asked.

"Not ever."

"Oh, motorcycles are in your blood, and you hate cars?" she teased as she opened her door.

"Let's go with that," he answered with a grin.

A flash of his expression from before at the market when that other biker caused problems jolted into her head and she blinked in reaction. He looked totally different.

"Who are you really?" she asked.

"I'm Talon. A Shadowridge Guardian and a mechanic. I also have some other roles in the MC."

"Like the Enforcer or the leg breaker?" she asked, watching his face to judge his reaction as she led the way to the kitchen.

"Kade's the Enforcer. You met him this morning. He's tough but fair. His Little girl loves him from here to the moon," Talon assured her as he set the basket on the counter and unloaded it.

"He has a Little girl?" Elizabeth echoed, taking Borscht when he handed the pink bear to her.

"He does. Her name is Remi. You'll meet her tonight."

Elizabeth tucked the stuffie in one of the stools at her counter before stowing her purchases away. Talon watched her silently as she finished placing everything in a bin in her fridge. When she closed the door, Elizabeth turned to meet Talon's eyes. "How does someone know if she's a Little girl?"

"Come here."

Taking her hand, Talon led her to her couch and sat down. He drew her onto his lap and lifted her into place when she tried to avoid sitting on his thighs. "I want to hold you, especially when we talk about important things."

After pressing a light kiss on her lips, Talon said, "Little girls are as varied as any other group of people. Bikers, librarians, religious people, police officers. You are the only one that knows if you're Little. If you crave the close relationship with your Daddy where you want someone strong in your life to take care of you, nurture you, and love you with every ounce of his mind, body, and heart, you might be Little."

Talon stroked the hair from her face that had escaped from

her ponytail. Meeting her gaze once again, he added, "Are you turned on by having someone else in charge? Maybe not all the time, but when you have free time from work and responsibilities, does the idea of leaving everything else in someone else's hands to make the decisions, deal with the annoyances of daily life, and protect you, make you feel good inside. Special?"

Forcing herself to be brave, Elizabeth nodded.

"Thank you for telling me the truth. Have you ever explored your Little side?" he asked.

"Not really? I mean, I like to read those books and I color sometimes."

"What's your stuffie's name?"

"Puff," she answered, not even hesitating because he asked so casually—like he already knew. "And now, Borscht."

"Is Puff a dragon?"

She nodded, feeling self-conscious.

"I'd love to meet him in a few minutes. Would you like to know what I would like to do for my Little?"

"Yes," she whispered.

"I would like my Little girl to do whatever she does as her job as long as she enjoys it—most days. When her day is over, she leaves everything at work and walks out the door. At home, she can relax and color, read, or watch a movie while I make dinner. After eating our meal together, we would spend time together doing whatever makes her happy."

"Wouldn't you rather do what you enjoy? Watch a game on TV? Go play poker with your friends?"

"I'm going to stop talking in general and concentrate on you. I think you're my Little," Talon stated firmly. "We will spend time with my MC brothers at the compound. There, you will enjoy the company of other Littles."

"Some of the Shadowridge Guardians are Daddies?" Elizabeth looked at him in shock.

"Most, if not all, are. Five have already found their Littles," Talon shared.

"Really?"

"They are absurdly happy together. We won't spend all our time with the Shadowridge Guardians. I have an apartment there, but I also have a house outside of town. I don't get there often, but it's a great weekend retreat," he shared.

"I'm glad you didn't go there this weekend," she confessed.

"Best decision ever." Talon leaned forward to kiss her lightly. Leaning back, he brushed her hair away from her temple.

After thinking for a moment, he added, "If it makes you happy to spend time with other Littles, I'll let you enjoy their company while I hang out with the other Daddies—supervising your gathering, of course."

"Do you think the others will like me?"

"Indubitably."

She laughed at his word choice and relaxed a bit more. Emboldened, she asked, "So being Little is all about games and playing?"

"No. Being Little often has an intimate component as well. For me, that's equally essential. I will make sure you feel good by making sure you are sexually satisfied and happy. Daddies care for all their Littles' needs."

Elizabeth felt her cheeks heat and knew she was blushing. When she looked away, he gathered her ponytail in his powerful hand and easily turned her head to meet his gaze. "I will take care of your health. No part of your body will be off limits to me. I will correct you when you endanger yourself, like today."

"A spanking?" she whispered, trying not to squirm on his lap.

"Among other things. Little girls need boundaries to help them make good choices."

She thought for a minute before saying, "I can be stubborn sometimes. I would act again in the same way to help that woman."

"That does not surprise me. Could you commit to calling me first before you put yourself in danger?"

"Maybe?" she hedged.

He arched one eyebrow and maintained eye contact with her.

"Okay, if you were my Daddy, then I'd call as soon as possible."

"Before interceding."

His stern tone made her hesitate before admitting, "It depends on the situation. I might not have time to call."

"If you endanger yourself, there will be consequences."

"You sound like you're my Daddy already," she said, bristling.

"Yes."

That simple word deflated her indignation. "How are you so confident?"

"There's something in you that calls to me. You feel like home. Go get Puff now. I'd like to meet him."

Thinking over his simple statement, Elizabeth allowed him to boost her to her feet. She walked slowly into her room and gently untucked Puff from his nesting spot. Cradling him against her chest, she returned to his side and hesitated. Should she sit back on his lap?

"Come here, Buttercup." Talon solved her dilemma by guiding her back onto his lap. "This is Puff?"

"It is. Puff is very fierce. Be careful. If he doesn't like you, he'll set you on fire."

"Wow. I hope he likes me. Hi, Puff. I'm very glad to meet you. Thank you for taking such good care of my Little girl." Talon held out a hand to the stuffie for him to sniff.

"Snort! Puff says you're a stranger."

"To him, definitely. But you and I know each other. Can you convince Puff to give me a chance?"

Elizabeth turned the stuffie to look at her. Looking into the dragon's amber eyes, she tried to reassure her long-time friend that Talon was okay. After several long seconds, the stuffie relented and snorted again.

"Puff is going to keep an eye on you, but he thinks you're good for me," Elizabeth reported.

"Thank you, Puff. Is it okay if I take Elizabeth out to eat now?"

The dragon nodded his head once.

"I'll go tuck Puff back into his lair," Elizabeth said. "I'll introduce Borscht to him later."

As she returned to the sitting area, Elizabeth paused. "Oh, I need to put on some makeup. I'm sorry I didn't do that sooner."

"No makeup, Little girl. I'd rather look at the real you," Talon assured her.

"But I look cuter in makeup." She hesitated.

"You look scrumptious now. Aren't you hungry?"

"I'm starved," Elizabeth admitted.

"Let's go."

Talon stood and ushered her out of the apartment. He paused in the doorway to make sure she had her phone and anything else she needed. When Elizabeth was ready, they returned to his motorcycle.

CHAPTER
FIVE

He could feel Elizabeth's body tense against his as they rode into the Shadowridge Guardians' compound. Taking a hand from the handlebar for a second, he squeezed one of her hands wrapped around his torso to reassure her. Pulling into his normal spot, he urged her to dismount before he put down the kickstand and turned off the bike.

Carefully, he helped take off her helmet. "You will have fun, Little girl. I promise."

Her lips were pulled in a straight line as she nodded. He could tell she didn't believe him.

"We can leave whenever you want. Just tell me 'pickled beets' and I'll know we need to fly out of here just like that jerk threw the jar."

That startled her out of the internal communication loop she had obviously created in her mind. "Pickled beets?"

"Can you remember that?" he asked.

Nodding, Elizabeth whispered, "I don't like beets. I'm going to give my jar to Janine."

"Me, neither. They taste like dirt. Or in that case, pickled dirt," he told her.

"You're going to give your jar away, too?" she asked, grinning at him.

"Definitely. Someone with no tastebuds here will love them."

Sweet giggles made him smile. "Turn around, Buttercup. Let me fix your hair. That helmet roughed you up a bit."

He pulled out her scrunchie and smoothed her hair into a high ponytail before replacing it. "Now all those tendrils of hair are out of your face. Ready to go meet everyone?"

"No. Talon, I'm scared."

"I know. It's okay, Buttercup. I won't go far from you, and no one is going to be mean here. Someone would smash them into the dirt for hurting a Little girl."

"Really?"

"Really. Can you be brave for me? It's only scary the first time."

"Okay. I'll try."

"Thank you, Elizabeth." He kissed her lightly before taking her hand to lead her to the front entrance and inside.

"Talon! And you brought someone with you to brighten up the place," a giant man greeted them.

"Hi, Bear. This is Elizabeth. She's mine."

"Hi, Elizabeth. Gabriel is making his highly coveted mac and cheese to go with burgers tonight. You chose a great night to come meet everyone."

"Hi, Bear. I'm glad to meet you," Elizabeth said politely.

Talon felt her scoot a bit closer to him and squeezed her hand. "You'll love the mac and cheese. Come meet Steele's Little girl. Do you remember meeting him this morning? He's the guy over there." Talon pointed out the president.

"Elizabeth!" A voice she obviously recognized from last night made Elizabeth look to the far corner of the open gathering area. Ink stood up and jogged forward. "Hey, I'm glad to see you."

"I'm glad to see you, too."

"We're on our way to meet some of the Littles," Talon explained.

"I saw several in the library off the kitchen," Ink told him.

"Thanks."

"You'll be here?" Elizabeth blurted.

"I will be. You're fine here. These guys would gnaw off their own arms before they'd hurt you," Ink assured her.

"Okay," Elizabeth whispered and squeezed Talon's hand. "Can you take me to see the ladies?" She wasn't quite ready to say Littles in front of others.

"This way." Talon guided her through the room.

People greeted them as they played pool, darts, and watched TV. There seemed to be burly guys everywhere. Maybe just because they took up so much room. Everyone was perfectly pleasant and pleased to meet her.

As they walked past the kitchen, Gabriel called, "Are you going into the library? Take that tray. I promised the Littles they could have an appetizer. Let me add one for Elizabeth."

When it was ready, Talon lifted the big tray of small cups of what looked like the gooiest concoction ever. He ushered Elizabeth into the small room and announced, "Hi, Littles. Meet Elizabeth. We bring appetizers for you."

"Elizabeth? What a pretty name. I'm Ivy," a petite brunette said as she set aside her book to stand up and approach.

She hugged Elizabeth before waving to the side as everyone rose to cluster in front of them. "Talon, why don't you put that tray on the table. Meeting Elizabeth is much more important than snacking. Just don't tell Gabriel."

A woman all in black introduced herself. "I'm Remi. My Daddy is Kade."

"Hi, Elizabeth. I'm Eden," the next woman shared. Her curly red hair bobbled around her face.

Talon couldn't help from smiling as each woman hugged his Little girl. From the look on her face, Elizabeth didn't quite know how to handle the friendly greetings, but she quickly adapted and hugged them back. He could tell they were so pleased to have her join the group.

"Hi. I'm glad to meet all of you, too," Elizabeth answered with a genuine smile that made her sparkle. "You are all Littles?" she whispered.

The three women nodded.

"Come sit down with us. We can eat our macaroni and talk. Are you okay if Talon hangs out just outside?" Remi asked. Her black-rimmed eyes contrasted greatly with her pink tiara. Elizabeth loved her unique style.

"Is that okay with you, Buttercup?" Talon asked.

Having all the eyes on her was a bit overwhelming but Elizabeth answered, "Yes. I'm okay."

She wanted a chance to talk to these women and alone would be better. Especially if they were nice.

"I'm right over there," Talon assured her. He pressed a kiss to her cheek before stepping just outside the small area.

"Come sit down, Elizabeth. You sit here where you can see your Daddy and he can see that you're okay," Remi suggested with a grin that told Elizabeth she had an inkling about what was going on in Elizabeth's mind.

"Thanks," Elizabeth said as she sat down in the indicated spot. Glancing out of the room, she saw Talon adjust where he stood talking to a couple of other men so he could see her clearly. She smiled to herself.

"He really likes you," Eden observed.

"He does. He thinks he's my Daddy."

"Have you had a Daddy before?" Ivy asked, leaning forward confidentially. "I had only read about them in books. Wow, are they even better in real life!"

"Really? That's me, too. I didn't know Daddies really existed," Elizabeth admitted as she relaxed, feeling instantly at home with this group.

"I had no clue, either," Eden chimed in.

"I did. But my father is a Shadowridge Guardian. I was raised here in the compound," Remi shared.

"That's so neat. They're not really all Daddies, are they?" Elizabeth asked.

"I haven't asked all of them, but I think they are?" Ivy guessed, lifting her shoulders up in a silent question. "Here. Eat the mac and cheese while it's hot." She passed out the cups and spoons and everyone took their first bite.

"Hot darnation! This is amazing!" Elizabeth said, taking another bite.

"Hot darnation?" Remi echoed and giggled.

It wasn't a mean giggle. It was pure mirth. The others joined in, including Elizabeth.

"Sorry. I really suck at cussing," she explained.

"I think you're really good at it," Ivy suggested. "You can't ever get spanked for saying hot darnation. Your Daddy will fall over laughing as he lifts his hand to swat your bottom."

"Do you really get spanked?" Elizabeth whispered, leaning in to talk confidentially.

"Some of us more than others," Eden said, nodding at Remi.

"I can't help it if my mouth says things my butt knows are bad." Remi defended herself.

It was quiet in the room for about twenty long seconds before they all burst into giggles. Elizabeth glanced at Talon and saw him looking at her with an eyebrow raised in concern. She gave him a thumbs up sign and a smile. When he nodded, she turned back to her new friends.

"Are you guys here often?" Elizabeth asked.

"I live here," Ivy told her before taking another bite.

"And you're with Steele, right?"

"Yes. So, Talon for you, hmmm?" Ivy asked.

"Is there something I should know about Talon?" Elizabeth asked.

"Nothing bad. He's always a jokester. I've never seen him with any woman more than once. Not that he's a player. He just doesn't get involved. Obviously, there's a reason for that. I'm glad to see him find the one he's looked for," Ivy answered quickly.

"He taught me how to dance last night," Elizabeth shared.

"How fun is that! He does have the moves. You should see him dance around the kitchen as he cooks. Talon turns Latin music on and goes to town. Last time, he let me and Carlee bang on empty pans like bongos to keep the rhythm with him," Remi said with a laugh. "Carlee isn't here tonight. There will be more Littles on other nights."

"I'll look forward to meeting everyone," Elizabeth stated and knew she was actually telling the truth.

"Did you wash your hands before eating?" a stern voice came from the doorway.

Ivy immediately froze and looked down at the finger she was using to swipe off the last of the cheese sauce clinging to the small cup's sides. "Hmm, no?"

"That's what I thought. Don't put that in your mouth," he warned with a steely-eyed look.

"Yes, Daddy."

Ivy carefully picked up one of the napkins from the tray and wiped her finger clean. "All better!"

Shaking his head, Steele joined Talon and the others.

"Tartar sauce!" Elizabeth suggested.

The quartet exploded with laughter that attracted the attention of those nearby.

Setting their empty cups on the tray, the Littles retreated to a more secluded spot on the floor to chat and get to know each other better. Elizabeth knew she'd never have to talk about pickled beets in the compound. It was a fun place.

CHAPTER
SIX

"'m glad you had a good time tonight. I know it was scary at first."

"I was being silly," Elizabeth assured Talon as they walked up the stairs to her apartment.

"Feelings are never silly," he said with a meaningful look. "It's okay to be scared in new places with lots of new people. The compound can be overwhelming with all the members and guests."

"Do you like living in a house all by yourself?" she asked. "Doesn't it get lonely after being around all the Guardians? You work there, too, right?"

"Let me answer the second question first. I do work at the cycle shop. I rebuild engines. Does it bother you being a Little girl for a blue-collar man?"

"I hadn't ever thought about it. What you do is much less important than what you are. I was married to a businessman and that didn't work out well for me," she shared.

"I want you to make sure you're running to me and not away from anyone like your ex-husband," Talon stressed.

"When I first met you, something clicked inside me. You felt righter than any man has ever seemed to me. I really didn't plan to date again. Then I ran into you."

"Good. I felt the exact same way. I don't ever plan on letting you get away."

That statement could have been threatening, but it wasn't. Warmth flared inside her chest as her feelings solidified.

"For your first question, my house is lonely. I enjoy spending time there, but I'm not there very much. It's outside of town. There's a big meadow behind my house. All sorts of wildlife gather there. It's calm and peaceful."

"Sounds beautiful."

"It is. Would you like to come visit tomorrow? You could bring Puff and Borscht to spend the night."

"I'll have to talk to my stuffies, but I think I'd like that. I have to work on Monday," she warned.

"Me, too. We'll set an alarm so you'll have time for breakfast before we both have to leave." Talon plucked her keys from her hand as they approached the door.

"It's a big step," she suggested as he unlocked her door.

"It's okay if you're not ready," he said, ushering her inside and closing the door.

Pulling Talon to the couch, Elizabeth waited for him to sit down before taking a seat on his lap. All the Littles had sat with their Daddies during dinner. It seemed perfectly normal now.

"I really feel like I got to know you better tonight. It was fun just hanging out," she shared.

"I'm glad. The Guardians are important to me."

"I can tell. They're like a big family. They just wear a lot more leather than the average family," she suggested, trying to look serious.

"You!" Talon pulled her forward to give her a giant bear hug.

"Sorry, I couldn't resist."

Feeling nervous, Elizabeth traced the tattoos on his forearm to give herself something to do. Gathering her courage, she whispered, "Can I ask you something?"

"Of course."

She peeked up at Talon's face and then focused back on his powerful chest. "The Littles said there are punishment spankings and good girl spankings. And that I should ask for a good girl spanking so I wasn't scared," she blurted.

He lifted her chin until their gazes met. "You can talk to me about anything, Buttercup. And they're right. There are different kinds of spankings. Are you worried about getting spanked?"

She nodded.

"Then I think a good girl spanking is a very wise move. Stand up, Elizabeth," he encouraged and helped her slide off his lap to stand in front of him.

Talon unfasted her jeans as Elizabeth did her best to stand still. It was so hard when the fear of the unknown rattled her. He pulled her jeans and panties down to her knees and she felt her face flame.

"Over my lap," he said gently.

Reassured by his tone, she allowed him to help her into position. She reached for the floor and discovered he held her dangling without the ability to brace herself with her toes or fingertips. Elizabeth jumped when his warm hand smoothed over her bare bottom.

"Such a beautiful baby."

"I'm not really a baby."

"Shhh," he said, reassuringly. "I'm attracted to your grown body as well as your Little spirit. Let me take care of you. Do you remember your safe word?"

"Pickled beets," she recited.

"Good girl. Spread your legs."

Tentatively, she relaxed her tensed muscles to move her legs apart just a small distance.

"More, Little girl. More."

Glad her face was hidden, Elizabeth couldn't imagine how much he could see. She felt her arousal growing. Being exposed to his gaze was tantalizing.

"That's my good girl," he praised and lifted his caressing hand from her skin.

She straightened her body as he landed the first swat on her bottom. The sting filled her mind, erasing everything else from her brain. She dropped back into position as a second and a third followed in rapid succession before his hand smoothed over her flesh. This time his flesh didn't feel as warm, and she knew the heat was building on her skin.

His touch moved lower over her upper thighs and across the exposed seam of her pussy. Instantly, the warmth radiating through her skin radiated to her intimate spaces. She squeezed her thighs together and yelped when a firmer spank landed.

"Thighs apart, Little girl."

Nodding quickly, she shifted back into position. Talon caressed her lightly again and she tried so hard to stay still. It was hard as she felt his touch now trailing her juices over her skin.

"I think my Little girl likes her spanking," Talon murmured softly.

Before she could react, he slapped her bottom several times without pause. Elizabeth bit her lip, trying not to cry out as heat built. Unable to squeeze her thighs together, she couldn't do anything to ease the arousal building inside her.

"Let me hear your sounds, Buttercup," he urged when he stopped to smooth over her skin again. This time, he dipped his fingertips into her pink folds. She shivered in reaction to the touch that was amazing but not enough.

"Please," she pleaded.

"Don't rush Daddy."

Several spanks later, he returned to play between her thighs. He dipped a finger into her wet opening. Zings of pleasure built inside her.

"Breathe, Little girl."

She sucked in a desperate breath, unaware that she had been holding hers.

"Good girl. You deserve a reward, don't you?"

"Yes!"

He shifted his fingers to brush over that small bundle of nerves at the top of her channel and circled it with a feather-light touch. When she pulled her legs together, he lifted his hand.

"Legs, Elizabeth. I can see I'm going to need some restraints for my Little girl," he said, without a hint that this was beyond the normal status for a couple.

Elizabeth squeezed her eyes together at the thought of being unable to move, being totally at his mercy. She forced herself to spread her legs and crossed her fingers, hoping he would follow through.

"Hmm, I think my Little girl likes the thought of being bound. I like that image, too, Buttercup," he growled.

He lifted his hand from her, drawing an automatic "No!" from her lips. His low chuckle did things to her. She felt his hand brush the side of her hip, tugging at something.

"Oh!" Elizabeth squirmed as she understood his movement. Talon was as turned on as she was. He'd needed to adjust himself inside his tight jeans. Her attention now focused on his body against her. She could feel his thick shaft pressing against her body.

He spanked her again until the heat in her punished skin seemed to radiate. Again, he paused to caress her intimately. Gasping, she held onto his muscular calf as the pain and pleasure blended together.

Suddenly, it was all too much. Pleasure exploded within her. Elizabeth jerked as waves of sensation flooded her body. His touch gentled against her, and she felt his fingers leave her intimate folds, trailing wetness against her skin.

Talon gathered her into his arms and lifted her effortlessly to sit on his lap. She gasped as her punished bottom touched his denim-clad thigh. Boneless, she rested against his broad chest and tried to gather herself as his hands slid over her back and arms.

"You are so responsive, Little girl. I'm very pleased with you."

"I've never felt like that," she whispered, curling her fingers into the soft cotton of his T-shirt to hold onto him.

"You've never had an orgasm?" he probed. She could hear the concern in his voice.

She peeked up at him. "Yes. But..."

"Only by yourself?" he suggested.

"Yes."

"Then the previous men you have been with are idiots," he told her bluntly.

"Maybe? I always thought it was me," she admitted.

"It's not you, Buttercup. You respond perfectly to my touch."

"Maybe you're just magic?" she suggested.

He chuckled, jostling her slightly. Talon grinned and smoothed his hands over her back and over her bare thigh. "You just remember that."

She nodded and laid her head back against his chest. "That spanking wasn't too bad."

"That spanking wasn't supposed to be. This was a good-girl spanking. You won't enjoy a bad-girl spanking. Bad Little girls don't get rewarded."

"You mean, no orgasm?" She struggled to understand.

"Exactly. Your bottom will be redder as well."

"I think I want to avoid those spankings."

"Definitely."

Silence fell between them as he rocked her on his lap. He smoothed the hair from her face and pressed a kiss to the top of her head. Her yawn broke the silence.

"Time for bed, Little girl."

Talon stood with her cradled in his arms and walked to her bedroom. There he set her on her comforter and smiled when she gasped at the feel of her hot bottom against the cool material. He efficiently stripped off her shoes and socks before tugging her clothes over her bare feet.

"Arms up," he directed.

Slowly, Elizabeth raised her arms. He pulled her T-shirt off and released the back of her bra.

As he slid the straps over her shoulders, he directed, "Little girls don't wear bras at home. It's not necessary."

"I always wear a bra," she said urgently as she tried to resist the urge to cover herself as he set the garments aside.

"Not with Daddy at home." Talon laid down the law. "You'll be more comfortable. A Little doesn't need to hide her body. Where's your nightgown, Buttercup?"

"It's under my pillow," she said, pointing at the pillow on the left of the double bed. Elizabeth wasn't quite sure about not wearing a bra, but she wasn't going to argue about it now.

Retrieving the nightshirt, Talon lowered it over her head and helped her thread her hands through the arm holes. "I love the fierce dragons decorating your shirt."

"I know. They're so cute. They look just like Puff." Elizabeth traced one of the cartoon dragons with a fingertip before looking up at him to ask, "I wonder if they make them with bears like Borscht?"

"We'll have to look. Later. Time to potty."

He lifted her off the bed and set her on the carpet. "You go while I clean up everything here."

Embarrassed, she walked quickly to the bathroom. When she flushed the toilet, she heard "Wash your hands" and realized she'd almost forgotten.

Quickly, she washed her hands. Talon walked in as she dried them on a towel. It seemed so intimate to be in the small bathroom together.

"Do you have a washcloth?"

"Of course!" She scrambled to find him one and handed a blue one over.

"Perfect."

He ran the water until it was warm and then wet part of the

small piece of fabric. "Come here, Buttercup," Talon directed, pointing to the large tile on the floor in front of him.

When she took her place, he washed and dried her face with the soft cloth. Throwing the damp cloth over his shoulder, he took Elizabeth's hand and led her to the bedroom.

"Lean over the bed," he directed, pointing at the freshly turned-down covers.

"Am I getting another spanking?" she asked, hesitating.

"No, Buttercup. No punishments if you follow my directions. Prop your elbows on the bed."

She bent over slowly, looking over her shoulder at him. As she moved into position, he grabbed the damp cloth. Puzzled, she waited.

"Hold still."

Talon lifted her nightgown to place a hand on the small of her back, holding her in place. He gently wiped her inner thighs and intimate folds, removing the last traces of her juices from her skin. She buried her face in her comforter.

"Daddies take care of their Littles completely, Buttercup." He finished by spreading her buttocks and brushing the terrycloth fabric between them.

"Talon!" she protested, trying to roll over as he paid attention to the small entrance hidden there.

"Daddy's in charge." He held her firmly in place as he finished. "I'll bring a thermometer over here to leave in your nightstand in case we're here in the evening."

"What? I have one of those things you press to your fore-head," she rushed to assure him, not quite sure what he was saying. "But I'm not sick."

"I'm glad, Little girl. I'll make sure you stay that way."

Releasing her bottom, he patted her fondly as he released his hold pinning her in place. "Little girls always have their temper-atures taken in their bottoms. It's more accurate. Besides, you need to get used to having things inserted here."

"Talon. Wait just a minute..." she began, turning over to look at him.

"Daddy is in charge. You don't think every one of those Littles you played with today receives attention to their bottoms frequently?"

She stared at him, unaware that her lower jaw had dropped in shock. He cupped her chin and lifted it back into place. "Daddies take care of their Littles completely, Buttercup. Give me a kiss. It's time for you to go to sleep. I'll lock the door as I leave."

"Borscht!" The pink bear popped into her mind.

"I'll go get him."

Talon was back in a couple of seconds. He tucked Borscht under the covers with Puff and Elizabeth. "Sleep, Little one. I'll come get you for breakfast at nine."

"Okay, Daddy."

He leaned close to give her a kiss that wiped everything out of her mind and made her wiggle in her toasty lair. "Night, Buttercup."

"Night, Daddy."

CHAPTER
SEVEN

"**D**addy's taking care of you, Buttercup."

Elizabeth woke with a hand between her legs and her face pressed to her pillow. Her covers lie crumpled around her elevated bottom as the echoes of the voice in her dreams dissipated.

She closed her eyes, desperate to recapture the dream. Elizabeth could picture herself restrained on her knees on an exam table. Talon stood behind her holding the thick thermometer in her bottom as he talked to someone. Having another person there made everything even more over the top. Her fingers worked furiously between her legs, trying to push herself into an orgasm.

Knocking at the door made her jerk upward to sit on her knees. *What time is it?* Holy farts! It was Talon.

"Coming," she called, grumpily acknowledging her frustration at not having time to make herself climax.

After making sure her nightgown was fully in place, she unlocked the door and scowled at the handsome man waiting there. "Hi. You woke me up."

"Sorry, Buttercup. Are you feeling okay?"

"No. I like sleeping in on Sunday," she answered grouchily, deliberately standing in his way to prevent him from entering.

"Let me have your hand," he requested.

Without thinking, she reached her right hand out before catching herself. Her fingers were probably still wet. Elizabeth quickly switched and substituted her left. To her consternation, he captured her right and lifted it to his nose. Frozen in place, she couldn't believe it when he licked her index finger.

"That's definitely your juices. Did I interrupt your play this morning, Little girl?"

"I don't know what you're talking about. I was asleep and your pounding woke me up," she answered with a glower.

"I don't believe you. Do you know what happens when you're flushed and you lie to Daddy?"

"Let me guess. A spanking?" she sneered.

"He first checks to see if you're running a fever."

Talon stepped forward and wrapped an arm around Elizabeth's waist to lift her feet off the ground. She gasped and grabbed onto his broad shoulders. Her hand closed over a leather strap blending into the leather of his vest. What had he brought?

He held her suspended in the air while he closed the door and locked it. After pressing a soft kiss to her hair, Talon whispered, "Good morning, sunshine."

"I am not sunny," she growled, more ticked off by the moment. Who was he to waltz in and just haul her around?

"I'd like you to let me down, please." Her tone for that last pleasantry did not make it polite.

He carried her over to the couch and tugged the strap of a leather satchel from under her fingertips. After setting it carefully on the cushion, he slid her down his body slowly until her feet rested on the carpet. Immediately, she tried to turn away, but Talon held her securely with that blasted arm around her waist.

"You are in a tizzy." He pressed his hand to her forehead and held it there for a few seconds. "A bit warm, but that could be because you're upset."

"Of course, I'm upset. You're hauling me around."

Talon completely ignored her words. "Let's see if I can figure this out. You overslept. You have traces of play on your fingers. You're grumpy."

"Oh, stop it," she hissed as he considered all the clues.

"I interrupted a dream, didn't I? And I was in it, wasn't I?"

"You are definitely full of yourself."

He tapped on his chin as if considering. "But were you full of me? I don't think so. You'd be much more satisfied."

He patted her bottom, erasing any protest about that arrogant statement from her mind. "We were talking about taking your temperature last night before I left. That's what you were dreaming about, wasn't it?"

Her eyes widened in shock. He couldn't know.

She quickly blustered, "Of course not."

"Then you won't mind if I take your temperature now to make sure you aren't sick?"

"No. I mean yes, I mind. No, you can't."

"You are so confused. I think we need to make sure you're feeling okay."

Talon walked backward, forcing her to take a few steps with him. He scooped her up into his arms and sat down on the couch. Before she knew it, he had flipped her onto her stomach and flipped the bottom of her nightie up to expose her bottom.

"Nooo!" she wailed.

He didn't answer her. Instead, he held her in place with one hand as he flipped open the bag he had brought. Withdrawing an oversized thermometer that made Elizabeth clench her bottom, he set it aside and pulled out a tube of lubricant to join the thick device. While she stared at those in disbelief, Talon gathered her hands at the small of her back.

"What? Let me go, Talon," she demanded, struggling.

"Daddies help their Littles' fantasies come true. There are

very few things off-limits between us. Is this a hard limit for you?"

Shocked by his direct words, Elizabeth told him the truth. "No."

"Am I totally off target thinking you were having an erotic dream about medical play?"

"No," she wailed, hiding her face with embarrassment.

"Am I not going to find you soaking wet and unsatisfied from your play before I got here?"

"Daddy," she whispered.

"Answer the question."

His tone was so stern, she shivered in reaction. When he placed one hand on her outer thigh, she caved. "Yes. I had a dream, and I woke up—touching myself."

"Thank you for telling me the truth, Little girl. I want you to always tell me your fantasies, and we'll try to make them come true, okay?"

"That's embarrassing," she protested.

"Who can you tell if not your Daddy? If you never tell me, we can't make them come true."

When she didn't answer that, he rubbed over her bottom and outer lips of her pussy. "You're soaked, Buttercup. No wonder you are grumpy that I interrupted it. Let's wake you up a different way now. Close your eyes."

She slammed her eyelids down and buried her face against the cushion.

"Good girl."

She could feel his fingers stroking down her sensitive inner thighs. Elizabeth spread her legs, heeding his silent request. Talon rewarded her with a quick dally between her legs that boosted her arousal back into overdrive.

She almost looked when she heard the click. What was that?

When he spread her bottom, Elizabeth froze. The feel of the cold lubricant made her shiver. He spread it over that small rosette. Just when she thought his touch on the nerve-laden entrance would drive her mad, he pressed a finger firmly into her tight passage. The air caught in her lungs as she tensed every muscle in her body at the invasion.

He rubbed the slick substance on the walls inside her until she was quivering from his touch. When his finger slid out, she knew what would come next. The sound of the case opening made her freeze once again. Seconds later, a cold, thick tube pushed into her bottom. He kept adjusting it, keeping her attention focused on the intruder.

Like I can think of anything else.

She felt him move to pick up something else. What had she missed? There was a short delay and then she heard a buzzing sound. Elizabeth definitely opened her eyes, but the sound was behind her now. She wanted to look but didn't want him to know she was peeking.

The rounded tip of a vibrator stroked over her pink folds before dipping further inside. He teased her soaked pussy with the device until her mind was overwhelmed by the sensations of him adjusting the thermometer in her bottom and the vibrations.

Talon seemed to sense just when she was about to erupt. As her body tensed before her climax, he lifted the vibrator from her body.

"Please," she begged.

"You have to wait ten minutes for the thermometer to register correctly," Talon answered.

"It's been ten minutes. I'm sure it has," she tried to convince him before humming audibly when he pressed the device back to her body. "Mmm."

"Not quite yet, Little girl. I'm watching the clock. Let's talk about something else to distract you. Where should we go today?"

She shook her head. Elizabeth could hear him talking but couldn't track his words enough to answer him. "Please!"

"Soon, Little girl. Maybe next time, I need to put you on your knees with your butt in the air to check your temperature. That will be exactly how I fuck your tight hole."

"Ahh!" A cry sprang from her lips as Elizabeth's entire world seemed to contract around her. She could feel her body shaking in reaction to the intense climax. Her fingers tightened around his hand that held her restrained.

"I bet you can come two more times before your ten minutes is up," he whispered softly from above her.

CHAPTER
EIGHT

lizabeth couldn't even look at him as they entered the popular restaurant known for its delicious brunch. Clinging to the hand of the powerful man beside her, she operated on automatic pilot. They were almost too late for brunch, but the hostess promised she'd get the kitchen to make their favorites for them.

"Scoot over, Buttercup," Talon instructed and slid into the booth next to her.

He wrapped an arm around her and tugged her close. Opening the menu, he read several special features off the menu as he rubbed her shoulder and arm. "What sounds best to you?"

"Not the strawberry one," she answered.

"Do you like bacon?"

"Bacon? Almost everyone loves bacon," she whispered, still feeling shaky from the pleasure he had shown her. "I'd eat it every day, but it's not good for you."

"There are times in life when you just have to say fuck it and eat the bacon. Bacon is delicious and a total day brightener. Why not include it in your life? Can you be brave for me and live on the edge?"

"Are we still talking about bacon, Talon? My mind is pretty discombobulated. I didn't know I could feel all that."

Talon leaned over to kiss her hair. "I got you, Elizabeth. You'll feel better when we get some food in you."

"I don't feel bad. Just mind-blown," she answered.

"Good girl. I can deal with mind-blown."

"Have you made your decision?" the server asked.

Talon ordered for them with Elizabeth barely paying attention to anything. When the waitress departed with their order, he hugged her close once again.

"You look very cute," Talon complimented.

"Thanks to you. I'm sorry, I'm not functioning well. That kinda blew my mind," she whispered.

After her orgasms, Talon had held her for a long time. She couldn't remember what he said but the tone of his praise remained with her. As did his statement that she wasn't allowed to touch herself without permission.

"I'm glad. Nothing is off-limits between us, Little girl. I expect you to tell me what turns you on and what you don't like."

"You're going to do that again?" she whispered, remembering him making a spot in her nightstand for the thermometer, lubricant, and vibrator.

"I'll check your temperature regularly," he told her without any hesitation.

It was as if it actually was something normal for a Daddy to do. She wished she'd gotten the Littles' phone numbers last night. They would answer her questions.

Meeting his gaze, she knew what they would tell her. Daddies are in charge. They take care of us.

"I enjoyed meeting the Littles last night."

"Good. They liked you."

"How do you know?" she asked.

"All the giggles coming from the library. And you were more comfortable around everyone when we had dinner."

"The big scary guys didn't seem so frightening when I saw them taking care of the others."

"I'm glad. The Shadowridge Guardians are fierce in their protection of people in our town. Don't forget that they will do almost anything to deal with people who endanger others."

She blinked at him. "Have you done bad things?"

"For the right reason? Yes."

The waitress appeared with a cup of coffee for Talon and a cappuccino for her. Picking up the frothy-topped hot drink, Elizabeth took a cautious sip and then another. The sugar and caffeine bolstered her energy and focus.

"That's good. Just what I needed," she whispered and took another drink. She looked over at Talon and knew from his smile that he'd ordered it for just that reason.

"Is there anything you don't know?" she asked before taking one more drink of the delicious mixture.

Elizabeth forced herself to set the cup down to show him he didn't know that much. His delighted chuckle made her smile as well. Everything was fun with him.

"You're so different," she said, looking at him.

"From other men you've dated? Or someone in particular?"

"My ex-husband."

"He changed after you were married?" Talon guessed.

"No. Not really. He was always a cold fish. I was stupid to marry him," she said, still too mind boggled to lie.

"I don't believe for a minute you were stupid. There had to be a reason you chose to marry someone."

"You're sweet," she said lightly before changing the subject. "What are we going to do today?"

"Tell me about him."

"You can't want to hear about my ex. It's history. I don't think about him."

"Tell me what I need to know."

Heaving a huge sigh, Elizabeth put her elbow on the table and propped up her jaw as she looked at him. "Davy was a guy I met in college. He was a loner. I talked to him because I was friendly to everyone. He assumed that meant I was interested in him. Foolishly, I never told him I really wasn't. And I married him when he asked."

"A guy you really weren't interested in?" Talon asked, his eyebrows drawing together in concern.

"It sounds really dumb in retrospect. Living it was a whole different thing. It just kinda happened. Five years later, I realized how stupid I was when he demanded we start having kids."

"You don't want kids?"

"Who knows? I'm thirty-two. Hopefully, I have more years to figure that out. I did know kids would force me to stay with Davy forever and that was way too long."

"So, you were smart to get out."

"Yes."

Elizabeth looked at Talon and blurted, "How old are you anyway?"

"Twenty-five."

"Good heavens. I was seven when you were born. I was already learning fractions and reading chapter books," she said, feeling old.

"Do you really think seven years makes a difference? It didn't this morning. It hasn't as we've spent time together," Talon pointed out.

"I figured my post-divorce wild fling would be with a silver fox," she admitted, shifting to take another sip of her cappuccino.

Talon's hand tightened over her thigh. "That's not happening."

She looked at him and smiled. "You've definitely been my reward for leaving. Oh, look! Here's our food."

Talon sat back to allow the server to place their plates in front of them. Looking at his selection for her, Elizabeth breathed in deeply. "Good choice. Bacon and golden French toast."

"I'm glad. You needed some protein and sugar to recover."

"Do you have some medical training?" She felt compelled to ask. Her cheeks were already turning red as this morning's activities refreshed in her mind.

"Not formally. Doc is our medical resource. He's taught all of us how to keep our Littles healthy. He also patches up the Guardians when needed."

"I'm not even going to address the first part," Elizabeth said, hoping her cheeks weren't fluorescent red. "Do you guys get in brawls?"

"Sometimes. It's not smart to cross the MC," Talon answered as he cut a bite of his omelet.

Elizabeth couldn't help from admiring the cheesy eggs with all the yummy fillings. She made herself focus on his words. "There are people stupid enough to mess with you all?"

"Try this," Talon directed, holding the bite to her lips.

Unable to resist, she opened her mouth. "Mmm. That's yummy!" she mumbled.

"Better than your French toast?" he asked.

Debating, she shook her head. "They're both good."

"Then we'll share."

He took a bite of her French toast and nodded. "Yours is good." He cut another bite of the golden bread and fed her.

Elizabeth looked at him with dancing eyes. Only a Daddy would share his breakfast with his Little and claim part of hers. She loved having a bite of this and a bite of that.

Picking up her fork, Elizabeth cut off a piece of his omelet and lifted it to his mouth. Without hesitating, he devoured it. She laughed out loud. Talon made everything fun.

CHAPTER
NINE

"What time do you need to be at work, Buttercup?" he asked from the kitchen as he did the evening dishes. The day had gone better than Talon would have ever dreamed. Spending time with his Little was magical.

Elizabeth set her crayon down and dug her phone from her back pocket. Able to see her screen, he watched her pull up her schedule. "I'm in cour... a meeting tomorrow. I'll have to leave here around six thirty to be organized."

"You're in court?" he asked.

She screwed her mouth in a bow and pulled it to the side as she thought. Talon waited to see if she'd tell him the truth or come up with something flamboyantly fake.

"Yes. I'm in court tomorrow," she admitted.

"What do you do in a courtroom? Are you the judge?"

"Oh, not yet," she popped off with before realizing what she'd said. "I mean—of course not."

"So, you're a lawyer? What's your specialty?" he asked, tossing the towel on the counter and coming to pull his chair at the table out. He whirled it around and sat down on it backward.

She hesitated for a moment. Talon was part of an MC. He admitted to doing bad things sometimes. Should she lie to him? Having him sitting right there looking at her convinced her to tell the truth. He'd obviously find out some day.

"Criminal defense," she admitted.

"So, you know a few things about the Shadowridge Guardians?" he asked.

"Not much. I've never been assigned a case that has anything to do with your group. I mean, I've seen the name. Not usually in a bad way. They escorted a battered woman into court to testify against her abusive husband."

"So, they were the good guys for that case?"

"Yes."

Elizabeth was quiet for a long time as she struggled to find the right thing to say. She didn't want her job to jeopardize this. Finally, she admitted, "I didn't tell you because I didn't know how you would react. Do you want me to leave?"

"No."

"That's all you're going to say?"

"You being a lawyer doesn't change anything for me. In criminal defense, you've stood up for people who need a champion and probably got a few people off even though you knew they were guilty as hell."

She nodded. He was completely right. Elizabeth loved the first and hated the second—but she did her job.

"You're my Little girl."

"Knowing this doesn't change everything?"

"Not for me. You know I'm a mechanic at a repair shop owned by a bunch of bikers with a kick-ass attitude. You didn't run away."

"You didn't give me a chance to run," she pointed out.

"I'm *never* going to give you that chance. I don't care what you do for *work* as long as you *enjoy life* with me," Talon stated firmly.

Elizabeth stared at him. Talon always cut straight to the chase. But she had to make sure he understood everything.

"My schedule is hectic. During a big case, my hours are crazy. Can you live with that?"

"I won't like it, but my hours can be weird as well."

"When you're involved in Shadowridge Guardian business?" she asked.

"When my brothers need me, I respond. The only person who ranks above them is you."

"Really? We haven't known each other for long," she pointed out.

"You're mine, Little girl."

She swallowed hard before admitting, "I feel good when I'm with you." Her face flamed red as she remembered just how good he could make her feel and watched a grin spread over his face.

"Not just when you're touching me," she said quickly. "Inside, I just feel better when we're together. It's like you're a missing piece that suddenly snapped into place."

"I like that, Buttercup. We fit well together."

"We haven't had sex. Maybe I'm crappy at it. My husband wasn't too excited," she blurted.

"You are amazing in my arms. Your ex-husband was a clueless bastard and is no longer part of your life. I'm sure he knew one position and sucked at everything but finding his pleasure."

Her mouth dropped open as she looked at him. *How does he know that?*

"There's an easy way to prove I'm right and you're wrong," Talon pointed out, scooting his chair closer to hers.

"What? You're going to whisk me away to the bedroom and test drive me?" she said. Could he tell her bluster was driven by self-consciousness?

"I'm going to make love to you like you should have always been taken care of."

She stared at him, allowing a small glimmer of hope to kindle in her heart.

"Come on, Buttercup."

He stood and held out a hand to pull her from her chair. When she stood, he bent down and scooped her over his shoulder.

"What are you doing?" she said, wriggling.

"Don't make me drop you," he warned, knowing he'd never drop her in a million years. To punctuate his words, Talon swatted her rounded bottom sharply.

At that quick taste of slight pain, he heard her quick inhale and knew he'd just started her engine. Damn her incompetent husband! Who could ignore the signs that she needed so much more than just missionary style in the dark?

At the doorway into his bedroom, Talon stopped to turn on the overhead lights. Immediately, she asked, "Can we turn those off?"

"I'm not making love to you in the dark, Elizabeth. I want to see every inch of your body and every bit of arousal on your face," he told her firmly as he walked to his large, four-poster bed.

Setting her feet on the carpet, he placed his hands on her hips and pulled her pelvis to his. "Making love to you is going to be a treat for all my senses."

He glided one hand up her arm, taking his time as he watched her focus on the simple move. Cupping her jaw, he whispered, "Touch."

She inhaled sharply and held her breath for what would come next.

"Taste." He captured her lips in a series of soft kisses that wooed her lips apart. Deepening the next exchange, Talon caressed her inner lips with the tip of his tongue and treasured the soft moan at the back of her throat that rumbled through her mouth. His hard kiss that followed made her fingers dig into his shoulders as she pressed her body against his.

Lifting his mouth from hers, he continued with soft kisses to her jaw and down the side of her neck. When he reached that sensitive spot where her shoulder began, Talon added, "Scent" to his list of treats. He inhaled deeply and paused, savoring the sweet fragrance that was uniquely hers.

"Talon," she said urgently.

"Daddy." He straightened to meet her gaze, putting sternness in his own.

"Daddy, please," she begged, clinging to him.

"I won't rush this, Buttercup. Daddy likes to play, too."

Talon glided his hands lightly over her ribcage to grasp the hem of her shirt. Pulling it upward slowly, he gave her time to lift her arms over her head so he could remove it. Looking over her beautiful body, he traced a finger over the swell of one petite breast. He cupped it in his hand and brushed his thumb across the tight nipple that pressed against the lace.

Her aroused moan was exactly the response he wanted. "Sound."

When she arched her back to push herself firmly against his hand, Talon traced the delicate garment's band to the back fastener with his other hand. Quickly unfastening it, he eased the garment from her body and tossed it aside.

Devouring the sight in front of him with his eyes, Talon whispered, "Sight. That's the last of my senses, Elizabeth. You appeal to all of them. Appeal, hell. You set my world on fire."

"Daddy!"

Not making her wait, he lowered himself in front of her to

slide off her leggings and panties. Scanning over her body as he stroked up her legs, Talon memorized her form. "Damn, Buttercup, you're this Daddy's dream."

He stood to cup her small mound and squeezed, feeling her wetness on his fingers. Talon loved how focused she was on him. Being the center of her world was an aphrodisiac like he'd never experienced before. Roughly, he adjusted himself in his now too-tight jeans. Her gaze followed his movement, and he watched her pink tongue peek out to wet her lips.

Clamping his control in force, Talon swept her from her feet and carried her to the side of the bed. He balanced her petite form against him as he ripped the covers down to the bottom of the bed. Gently placing her against the pillows, he stepped back and allowed his eyes to devour the gift that awaited.

Reaching over his head, Talon yanked his T-shirt over his head and tossed it away. He watched her focus on his chest and tribal tattoos. Unfastening his jeans much more carefully to avoid his fierce erection, Talon enjoyed her look of shock as his cock burst free. He paused for a moment to allow her to look, enjoying her heated stare. It struck him how much his Little's fascination with his body made its mark on his heart. Her desire matched his own.

He couldn't wait too long. His prize waited for him. Forcing himself to think ahead, he grabbed a pack of condoms from the nightstand and ripped it open to pull out the string of packets.

"Got big plans?" she whispered.

Delighted by her teasing, he growled, "I may never let you out of my bed. I'm safe, Buttercup. Tested last month and haven't been with anyone since."

"Me, too. I tested after my divorce. Just in case."

"That's my wickedly smart Little girl. Now, I plan to make you forget everything."

At her nod, Talon propped one knee on the bed to lean over her. Running his hand over her shoulder and down to her fingers, he linked his with hers to squeeze lightly. "Damn, Buttercup, I am a very lucky Daddy."

She raised her free hand to trace over his chest and lower. Talon trapped her hand against his abs. "You don't have permission to touch Daddy."

"I need permission?" she repeated, lifting her gaze to meet his.

"Daddy's in charge."

He waited as a long second passed until she nodded and slid her hand from under his to lay higher on his chest. "Good girl."

Releasing her fingers, Talon lowered himself to his elbow, supporting his weight as he stretched out on the mattress beside her. Her hands played over his skin, touching and teasing him. He wrapped a hand behind her head and held her steady as he lowered his lips to hers.

The heat building between them flared hotter as their bodies blended together. Her softness molded to his muscular physique, making Talon's cock twitch against her. When he lifted his head, she bit her lip.

"What's wrong, Buttercup?"

"I don't think you'll fit," she whispered, waving a hand down his body.

"We'll fit together perfectly. You were made to be mine. I'd never hurt you," he promised.

Some of the worried lines on her forehead dissipated, but Talon could read her lingering apprehension. "I promise."

Elizabeth nodded slowly, and he felt the tension ease from her body. "Thank you for trusting me, Little girl."

Rewarding her with another kiss, Talon took his time. Rushing this wasn't an option. Stroking his hand over her body, he searched for those sensitive spots that made her breath hitch or brought a smile to her face. He couldn't resist the allure of her pert breasts. Each a perfect handful, Talon cupped one.

"Do you taste sweet here, too?" he asked before capturing her small, pink nipple between his lips. Tasting the tip with his tongue, Talon rolled it lightly and then harder between his lips. Her moan and the nails biting into his shoulders clued him in that his suspicion she enjoyed a bit of pain was completely on target.

Opening his mouth, he sucked her tender flesh into his mouth. Talon moved slowly backward, increasing the pressure before releasing her suddenly.

"No!" burst from her lips and he smiled against her skin as he moved to treat her other breast exactly the same way.

He stroked a hand down her abdomen. Her body was perfectly formed, and he loved her softness. Reaching her trimmed adult hair, Talon tugged it lightly, drawing a moan from her lips. "Daddy will remove this tomorrow."

"Am I going to see you tomorrow after work?"

Her hesitant question made him look back to meet her gaze fully. He struggled to understand that other men, including her dunce of an ex-husband, might not have craved her as he did somehow. "You're going to see me every morning, afternoon, and evening, Buttercup, if I have my way. You're in my blood now. I won't ever get enough of you."

His fingers dipped into her wetness and she stilled. He remembered exactly where and how she liked to be stroked. Talon gave her what she wanted while searching for new delights.

She was so responsive. Leaning over her once again, he pressed a hard kiss to her mouth and loved her passionate answer. Talon scattered kisses over her body. He treasured her wiggles of pleasure and hands tightening on his body or tugging his hair.

Pressing two fingers into her pussy, he rotated his hand to stroke his thumb over that small bundle of nerves hiding at the top of her entrance. Her body froze as a wail escaped her lips before shaking as waves of contractions squeezed his fingers.

"Daddy!"

"I'm right here, Buttercup."

He moved his fingers inside her body, extending her pleasure as he stretched her in preparation for his cock. She was soaked, but he would need to go slow—even if it killed him.

When he felt her moving against his hand as if seeking more, Talon grabbed a condom and sheathed himself quickly. The feel of his own hands on his body made him realize how much control he would need to gather.

Caging her under him, Talon cradled one side of her face. He kissed her deeply, enjoying her flavor and response as he lowered his pelvis to hers. Guiding her petite leg around his waist, Talon slid his shaft against her wet pussy. The gliding contact drew a moan from deep within her.

Shifting, Talon placed his cock at her entrance and pressed slowly inside. When he felt her fingers tighten on his shoulders, he reversed his movement.

"No!" she protested, trying to keep him close.

"Shh, Elizabeth," he said, meeting her gaze directly. "We're going slow. Your body needs to adjust to me. I don't want to hurt you. Daddy's in charge."

"Daddy's in charge," she repeated before requesting, "Can we try again?"

"Buttercup, we're going to try over and over. And when we finish, we're going to try it all again," he promised her as he pushed back into her.

Her body relaxed around him, and Talon slid further inside. He watched her eyes roll back as his cock brushed over sensitive places inside her. Changing his angle slightly, he felt her fingernails bite into his shoulders.

"More," she whispered.

Holding himself together by sheer will, Talon eased in and out of her body several times slowly. When his pelvis met hers, he kissed her hard. "Mine."

"Yours," she promised.

Rocking in and out of her tight wetness, he knew nothing would ever feel this good. This woman was his everything. He experimented to find the best way to please her. Talon loved the sound of her breath coming ragged from her chest as he pushed her toward pleasure over and over.

The room warmed with their passion. Sweat dampened their skin, alluring him with her feminine scent. Elizabeth lapped her tongue along one of his tattoos, threatening his control like no one ever had. He tangled his hand in her hair and tugged, tilting her lips up to meet his. The moan of passion that whispered from her lips carved itself in his memory.

He treasured every moment buried deep within her. The feel of her coming around his cock was pure heaven. He never wanted this to end but knew he couldn't continue to hold on. "One more time, Buttercup. Come with Daddy," he urged.

"Please," she whispered, holding on to him for strength.

Talon increased his speed, targeting her most responsive spots as he caressed her with a hand. Teasing, he moved his hand lower and lower until it pressed between them. He brushed his fingertip over her clit and felt her shatter around him.

Loosening his control, he stroked into her, extending her pleasure until his body exploded. He poured himself into the condom as he roared his release into the room.

When their bodies calmed, Talon eased from her body, loving the gasp of protest that whispered from her lips. He dealt with the condom quickly while maintaining contact with her. He couldn't be separated from her.

With her gathered in his arms, Talon smoothed the covers over her shoulders and tenderly hugged her to his body. "Oh, you please me, Little girl."

Her sigh of "Daddy" before she tumbled into sleep made him smile.

Damn, I love her.

CHAPTER
TEN

"Wake up, Little girl. It's time to jump in the shower," a deep, sexy voice cajoled her.

"What? Oh, crap!"

Instantly, Elizabeth was in work mode. She scrambled away from his warm body to jump out of bed. Instantly embarrassed to find herself naked in front of him, she waved self-consciously at the handsome man grinning at her and fled for the bathroom.

When she emerged, the water was already running in the large walk-in shower. Focused, she headed for that. Powerful arms wrapped around her waist and pulled her against his hard body.

"Wave good morning at me?" he teased before lowering his mouth to press a blistering kiss to her lips.

Instantly, she battled the temptation to fall under his spell versus the need to be ready for work. Regretting her actions before she even moved, Elizabeth pushed against his chest.

"Talon, I have to get to work."

"Daddy," he corrected her. "Call me Talon in public if you wish, but when we're alone…"

She interrupted him. "Daddy. I can do that. Now, Daddy, I

need to get less" —Elizabeth waved a hand over her body—
"sexed up. I smell like you."

"I like you smelling like me. Give me a kiss and I'll let
you go."

Rising on her tiptoes, she gave him a fiery hot kiss that
rivaled the one that almost derailed her earlier. They were both
breathing heavily as their lips parted. Talon stepped back,
clearing the path to the shower.

"Go."

Walking fast to the shower before she could convince herself
they could have a quicky before work, Elizabeth glanced over
her shoulder to find him watching her derriere as she walked.
Grinning, she turned back and dived into the shower. Her hair
was a mess, but it would take too long to dry. She'd have to pull
it into a bun.

As she dipped her face into the water to wash it off, she
heard a second showerhead sputter to life. Turning to see Talon
standing with his head under the spray and water coursing over
his chiseled body, everything inside Elizabeth heated up. The
moan that escaped her lips drew his attention.

"Work, Little girl. Playtime tonight," he promised as he
scanned her body with equal enjoyment. "Whoops, we forgot
one thing."

She knew immediately what he meant as he picked up his
shaver and dispensed liquid soap into his hand. Talon lowered
himself to kneel on the tiled floor. Without saying a word, he
completed the job he'd promised to do before turning her body
back into the spray to rinse off the lather and her adult hair.

The spray on her now sensitive skin made her shiver. She felt
him rise to standing behind her and held her breath as he
pressed himself against her to lay a kiss on her shoulder before
moving away.

Mentally shaking herself to put the thought of shower sex out
of her mind, Elizabeth tried to erase the feel of his thick, erect
cock trapped between their bodies. Catching herself, she filed

that sensation into a special part of her brain. She definitely didn't wish to forget that.

Forcing herself to shower, she tried not to notice the small love marks that were scattered over her body. Talon was a demanding lover and she remembered how he'd left each one and the effect on her body. They would all be covered under her clothes, but she would know they were there.

A short time later, efficiently dressed and wearing her professional face, Elizabeth stepped into her low pumps. "Can I leave all my stuff here?" she asked before adding, "I mean if I'm staying tonight?"

"There's no doubt that you're sleeping in my bed tonight. I have plans for you."

"Plans?" she asked, arching an eyebrow at him.

Talon walked forward to turn her to face the bed. Moving behind her, he didn't crush her to his body but simply allowed her to feel his heat. "Look at the headboard," he ordered.

Unsure where this was going, she focused on the carved wooden bed. "What about it?"

He leaned close to press his mouth to her ear and growled, "Daddy's going to drill a hole in the carving to add a hook to hold your hands restrained over your head. I'll add more to the supports on the foot board so I can tie your legs spread widely apart. Then I can do anything I want to your sweet body. And you're going to love every minute of it."

She shivered against him, seeing that picture vividly in her mind. Tied spread eagle to the bed, he would have access to everything. She wouldn't be able to stop him.

Elizabeth turned to look at him. She allowed her face to reveal her inner desires. "How am I going to function today?"

"Work mode, Buttercup. Focus on your tasks and get them done. I'll be here when you get off work."

"It may be late."

"I'm not going anywhere. What's a four-digit number you remember easily?" he asked.

"Nine, six, four, two."

"That means something?" he asked curiously.

"During my probationary period as a lawyer, I won nine cases, settled sixty-four, and lost two."

"I take it that's a good record?" Talon asked.

"Those two still irk me."

"Of course, they do, Buttercup. Nine, six, four, two. It's your code to the front door. Come home as soon as you can. I need to take care of you."

"Yes, Daddy."

Elizabeth rushed to the door with her purse and keys. "I need Borscht and Puff. I'll stop on my way home to get them."

"Give me your key. I'll pick up your stuffies," he said without missing a beat.

As she handed it to him, he exchanged the key for a smoothie. "Drink this on the way. You need energy, Little girl. Is it okay for me to make a copy?" he asked, holding up the key.

"Yes. And thank you, Daddy," she answered, lifting the cup toward him with a grateful look. Elizabeth stepped forward to kiss him lightly so she didn't mess up her lipstick before forcing herself to dash out the door. The last thing she saw before stepping out the door was a small electric drill and several eye hooks lying on the entryway table.

How was she ever going to concentrate today?

Talon missed her immediately as he watched her get into her slick sports car and drive away. Suddenly, he wanted to see her in lawyer mode. Maybe she'd let him come watch a trial someday.

The drilling only took a few minutes. He placed the holes so they were disguised in the carving. The tether points could be removed if needed to disguise their intent. He took time to straighten up the house and even threw some things into the crockpot so dinner would be ready when she got home. Talon repeated that word to himself. Home. Somehow having Elizabeth under his roof transformed it from a house to something more.

Finally, stepping into his work boots and dragging a Shadowridge Guardians Motorcycle repair shop T-shirt over his head, Talon got ready for his day. As he took one last look around, Talon happened to see a marker on his dresser. Grabbing it, he wrote stuffies on the inside of his wrist where it might survive all the times grit and dirt were wiped off his hands. He was not going to forget Puff and Borscht. A second thought drifted through his mind and he wrote helmet and bear.

In a few minutes, he was out the door and on his bike. It was a beautiful morning filled with idiots rushing through traffic to get to their jobs on Monday morning. As usual, Talon was alert to everything happening all around him. He was used to negotiating the heavy traffic. Thanks to his Shadowridge Guardians MC vest, most people backed off and gave him some room.

The roar of a motor sounded behind him, and Talon looked over to see Atlas pulled up next to him. Pleased to see a fellow Guardian, Talon extended his hand down to his leg in a motorcyclists' greeting. Atlas returned the gesture and the two continued down the road, watching out for each other.

The number wizard had stabilized the books and gotten the MC back on track after the previous treasurer had played fast and loose with the club's money. He'd asked Talon to audit the accounts on a monthly basis so the members could rely on two Guardians to take care of the club's money. Talon had learned a lot from Atlas and enjoyed getting to know him.

When they exited off toward the Shadowridge compound, the traffic disappeared. Not many executives were headed to the industrial part of town. Pulling up to the garage, they backed their bikes into parking spots with the ease of people who had maneuvered bikes for years.

"Hey, Atlas! How was your weekend?" Talon called.

"Good," the more gentle-faced man replied.

Talon knew better than to think the guy who looked most like a boy scout in the Shadowridge Guardians was a weak link. He'd seen Atlas help defend the MC in a number of skirmishes. He'd take the man's massive biceps on his side every time.

"Carlee was upset she missed meeting your Little girl. Elizabeth, right?"

"Yes, Elizabeth is mine. I hope Carlee is okay?" Talon asked.

"Doc recommended I give her a treatment for her tummy. It worked well and she felt much better," Atlas shared.

"I need to get with Doc. He's amazing at keeping the Littles feeling their best."

"I have a feeling there are some Littles that wish he didn't know so much," Atlas said with a laugh.

Talon grinned. "I'm sure there isn't a truer statement than that. Do you need me today?"

"Tomorrow, I'd love to have you audit the books. Check the schedule and see if you could be available at two," Atlas requested.

"I'll block out some time."

The two men walked inside and parted ways. Atlas went into the clubhouse to attack the paperwork and Talon headed into the shop.

First things first, Talon asked, "Do we have any small adult helmets in stock?"

"Yep, check the right side of the shelf. I stocked up on sizes so everyone can fit their Little girls. No matter what size they are," Kade called back.

"In my dreams," Saint called as he threaded a new ignition cable into place.

"I didn't think mine would ever show up either," Talon admitted. "And then there she was."

He grabbed a smaller helmet, approving of the safety rating Kade had chosen to order. After marking it on his sheet to be subtracted from his pay, he collected a cream-colored bear from the bin to replenish his saddlebag. Noting he had a few minutes left before his office shift started, he jogged out to his bike and squeezed in the new helmet. He'd check to see if the new protective gear fit Elizabeth better and then remove his current spare. The bear, of course, got its own saddlebag to stretch out in.

CHAPTER
ELEVEN

D ead tired, Elizabeth walked out of the courthouse toward her car. There were a few people in the area, so she didn't really notice that the parking lot was basically deserted. Her thoughts focused on the best questions to ask the witness scheduled for tomorrow.

"Hey, it's Talon's bitch," a familiar voice sneered.

Recognizing the biker from the outdoor market, Elizabeth stared at him directly. Acting fearless usually worked to dissuade anyone from messing with her. When he stepped directly in front of her, she tried to go around him. When he moved again to stand in her way, she lifted her phone to take a picture of him. In a couple of clicks, she'd forwarded it on.

"What are you doing, bitch? Want to remember me?" He glowered at her.

"Just registering a picture of you with the police in case you think bothering me is a good idea. The courthouse parking lot is protected and secured by officers. They should be here within a few seconds," she answered, presenting an unruffled expression.

Elizabeth could stand toe to toe with bad guys all day long until they backed down. Then she'd go home and have a panic attack in private before building her walls back up for the next time.

"I can do a lot of damage in a few seconds," he threatened.

"On video," she countered, nodding at a camera posted nearby.

"You've got an answer for everything, don't you, Miss Lawyer. You know that Guardian scum you're hanging out with isn't going to be around for long."

"I don't think he's going anywhere," Elizabeth corrected and forced herself not to relax as she heard one of the security guards call her name.

"I'm over here!" she yelled, despite the biker's aggressive step forward.

"Ms. Sinclair, do you need an escort to your car?" the out of breath guard asked, stepping up to her side with his hand cupped over his taser.

"Yes, Tom. I'd appreciate it."

Elizabeth deliberately took a step to the side away from the furious threat in front of her. She noted the name on the jerk's vest—Vengeance. It seemed like someone was easily insulted and determined to get back at someone.

"Ms. Sinclair, are you okay?" the guard asked as they moved away from the biker, with Elizabeth taking a careful position on his left away from the taser he still hovered over.

"I'm okay. Thank you for the escort," Elizabeth answered, not allowing any of her fright to show in her even tone.

"Of course. You can stop at the desk and request someone walk you to your car in the future if you're coming out late," he informed her as they reached her car.

"Thank you. I'll remember that."

Sliding into her car as if it were any other night, Elizabeth was aware the biker group was watching her. As she started her engine, she noticed them straddling their bikes. She backed out cautiously and drove to the exit of the parking lot.

To her dismay, the bikers drove over the curb bypassing the

exit and dropped into place behind her. Elizabeth fumbled for her phone she'd set in the cup holder. The bikers sped up, starting to move along the sides of her car. She put both hands back on the wheel and stepped on the gas.

Crossing her fingers, she asked her phone to call Talon. Almost immediately, she could see the phone call processing on her dashboard.

"Hi, Butter…"

"They're surrounding my car." She interrupted his greeting. Immediately, she heard rustling and knew he was on his feet.

"Who?"

"Those Devil guys. What do I do?"

"Where are you?"

"About two miles from the courthouse on Broadway."

"You're closer to the compound than you are to the police station. Take a right at the next light."

Swerving into the lane, she hoped she'd lose the bikers but they reacted too fast. "I made it. They're still with me."

"They're going to stay with you. It's okay. You're almost there. Try not to stop at any lights." He stayed calm, but in the background, she could hear him slam a door behind him.

"How do you know where I am?"

"I'm tracking your phone now," he explained. "I'm on my way to you."

"What?"

"You can yell at me later," Talon pointed out.

"I don't think I'll make this light. It just turned yellow."

"You'll make it. Don't slow down unless you have to," Talon ordered. His motorcycle engine flared into life, sharing the sound through his phone.

"You're going to hear Kade's voice," Talon warned.

She could hear the phone connecting and then a deep voice answered, "Talon?"

"I made it, Talon," Elizabeth said quickly.

"Kade, you're looped into a call with Elizabeth. The Devils

are after her baby blue Charger. She's about six miles to the west of the compound, coming in on thirty-seventh."

"I'm sending some guys out to meet you, Elizabeth. Don't slow down when you come into the compound. Pull directly into the repair shop. We've got you," Kade told her. "Storm, Faust, Ink! Get on your bikes. Protect a blue Charger. Talon's Little. Coming west on thirty-seventh."

"Little girl, I'm coming as fast as I can," Talon told Elizabeth. "Keep telling us what's happening."

"They're creeping up next to the car. I'm going as fast as I can on this road," she said, hearing the panic in her own voice.

"Swerve to the right. They'll move," Talon ordered her.

"What if I hit them?"

"You won't."

A fist hit the side of her car, and another landed on the window. Fright skewered down her spine. "They're hitting the car!" she yelled.

"Swerve now, Little girl!" Talon's voice sounded tense.

Gritting her teeth, Elizabeth swerved over the dotted line. The motorcyclists fell back. "That worked," she breathed in relief.

"Good girl. Can you see the motorcycles coming toward you?"

"Not yet. I'm at a curve in the road."

"Keep your speed up. They're almost to you," Talon assured her.

"There they are! The Shadowridge Guardians! I recognize Ink's bike!" Elizabeth shut up to concentrate on making it safely around the bend at her speed. The next time she looked in her rearview mirror, the Devil's Jesters had slowed down.

"Talon! They're dropping back. They're turning around."

"Watch the road in front of you," Talon urged.

"The Guardians are all behind me now."

"They'll escort you back to the compound safely. Take a deep breath. I'm almost to you," Talon promised.

"I'm going to need a hug," she whispered, not caring that Kade was still on the line.

"You're going to get more than that," Talon promised.

In what seemed like a blink of time, Elizabeth drove her car into the compound. Shadowridge Guardians lined her route, ready to provide protection. She followed their directions and pulled into an empty bay in the repair shop. Immediately, a large man she recognized as Remi's Daddy was at her door to open it.

"Unlock the door, Little girl," Kade said softly when she just sat there in shock.

Looking at him without processing his words, Elizabeth had never been so happy to see a fierce-looking man in her life.

"Little girl, I can't get you out of there until you click the button for me," he said softly as the other men gathered close but didn't swarm the car.

In all her time working with some of the hardest criminals in the city, Elizabeth had never been so frightened. She shook her head. "I can't do it."

"You can, Elizabeth. You're safe now."

A roar of a motor made her hands tighten around the steering wheel. She watched Kade's face to see if something awful was happening. He nodded at someone and turned back to look at her through the glass.

"Your Daddy's here, Little girl."

Looking in her rearview mirror, she saw him swing his leg over the bike. Ink stabilized it for him as Talon ran toward her, yanking at the buckles on his helmet. Elizabeth reached for the door release and tried to get out, but something was holding her in place. She panicked, trying to scramble out of the car.

"Whoa, Buttercup. You're okay. Let Daddy help." Talon leaned in the car to wrap an arm around her body. Holding her tight against him, he used his other hand to release the seatbelt she'd fought with.

"Let's get this off," he explained when she clutched him desperately as he shifted slightly back.

Finally, he scooped her out of the car and hugged her tight against his body. Immediately, Elizabeth wrapped herself around him. She never wanted to let go of him. His hands smoothed over her back as she buried her face against his neck.

"Little girl. You scared all of us."

"Sorry," she mumbled against his skin. "Why?"

"I don't know, Buttercup, but I'm going to find out. This ends now," Talon assured her.

"You stay with your Little. I'm going to take a few guys to pay a visit to the Devil's Jesters. Stay here where we can protect you." Kade's voice was steely. Elizabeth had never heard that tone from the Enforcer of the MC. She understood now how Remi's Daddy had earned that position. His next words were directed to her in a completely different tone. "Elizabeth, if you can tell us what happened that will help."

Trying to pull herself together, she leaned back slightly from Talon's body. "It was that Vengeance guy. They were in the courthouse parking lot when I got out of work. He wouldn't get out of my way even when I tried to step around him. I took a picture of him and sent it to the guards at the front door. Someone came to help me."

"So, they followed you out of the parking lot to mess with you when you were out of the reach of the security guard?" Kade asked, his tone getting even harder.

"Yes. They partially surrounded my car and beat on it. Is it okay? Did they leave dents?" she asked, pushing away from Talon's body and dropping her feet toward the ground.

"I don't see any damage, Talon," Breaker reported.

"Your car's okay," Talon assured her as he relaxed his arms to allow her to slide down his body to stand. "Go look and reassure yourself."

"Come with me?" she asked.

"Of course."

Breaker shined the light he held in his hand along the sides of the car on both sides, allowing her to inspect it herself. Elizabeth didn't touch the paint. The car would have to be washed before she did that.

"This was the same jerk from the market?" Kade asked.

"Yes."

"Any idea why he was at the courthouse?" Kade questioned her.

"He's a criminal? I don't know but I'll find out tomorrow," Elizabeth promised.

Steele turned to look at the MC members gathered around. "Doc, Faust, Storm, King, Bear, saddle up. We're going to pay a friendly visit to the Jesters."

"Friendly?" Kade questioned. "I'm coming, too."

"Of course, you are," Steele said as if he knew he didn't even need to say Kade's name. "We're going to start friendly."

CHAPTER
TWELVE

Talon drew her away from the other club members and sat on a bench outside the repair facility. Scooping her up to sit on his lap, he rocked her slowly. "I'm sorry, Buttercup."

"I'm used to people threatening me at work. I've never had someone come after me outside of the courthouse. And why? I don't know this guy. I've talked to him twice now and he's just a bully."

"The Devil's Jesters are a club very different from ours," Talon told her, brushing her hair back from her face.

"They're all violent assholes?" popped out of her mouth.

Talon chuckled. "We have our share of that type, too. The difference rests in our focus. The Jesters thrive on chaos. The Guardians thrive on protection."

"They protected me tonight. I was never so glad to see a horde of motorcycles speeding toward me as I was tonight."

"I'm glad. I'm sorry I couldn't get there faster." Talon hugged her hard and looked so sad, Elizabeth couldn't help but jump in to take away the guilt he felt.

"I bet you were at your house making dinner for us. You

were trying to take care of me that way. Who knew this jerk was going to show up at the courthouse?"

"I do have some cheesy potato soup in the crock pot."

When her stomach growled in response, Talon asked, "Did you eat the lunch I sent with you?"

"I didn't have time. My day was packed. A case spilled over into my lunch break."

"Shall we go home and feed you? Or would you rather stay here for a bit longer? Gabriel or Bear will have food ready for the MC."

"I want to go to your house."

"Let's go."

In a few moments, they departed through the gates with Talon following Elizabeth home. When he escorted her into his house, she sighed with pleasure.

"I could love this house," she admitted, shrugging out of her blazer and folding it carefully over the couch.

"I'm glad. I'm hoping you will decide to make your home here with me," he told her as he took her things from her hands. "That's too much to think about tonight. Come eat."

Eagerly taking his hand, Elizabeth allowed him to lead her over to the table. She could tell how he'd literally dropped everything to come after her. "You broke a bowl," she said, pointing to the shards.

"I did. You were more important than the bowl. I didn't like these anyway," he told her. Talon dropped a kiss on her head before efficiently cleaning up the mess and dishing up a big bowl of soup for them.

When they were settled at the table with Elizabeth on his lap, he blew on the surface of the hot soup before holding it to her lips. "Here, Buttercup. Let's fill that tummy."

After swallowing, Elizabeth looked at him gratefully. "That's wonderful."

"Do you like oyster crackers?" he asked, opening a bag of small, round crackers meant to go in chowders.

"By themselves. They're fun to snack on."

"Here." He poured a few on a small plate for her and pushed it close.

After popping two in her mouth, she chewed happily as he tried the soup. "These are good."

"Let me see." He snagged a few from her plate before she could pull it away.

"Mine, Daddy. Get your own."

"You won't share with Daddy?" he asked with a hurt expression.

She thought about it for a minute and nodded. "I'll share. Just don't eat them all."

"I promise, Buttercup. Here, eat some more soup."

Talon's phone rang, making her jump. He finished feeding her the bite before picking up the device. "Talon here," he answered.

Elizabeth listened carefully, trying to hear. She signaled Talon to put it on speaker, but he shook his head no. Pissed, she pulled the bowl of soup in front of her and ate without him. This was *her* life. She was entitled to know what was going on.

When he finished the call, she pushed the soup back toward him. "I'm finished."

"Let me tell you what happened," Talon began.

"Whatever you want to do. I know it's Shadowridge Guardians business," she answered airily as she stood up and snagged the bag of oyster crackers to take with her.

"Come here." Talon pulled Elizabeth back onto his lap.

"You're going to spill the crackers," she warned.

"I don't care about the crackers. I care about you," he said firmly, holding her in place.

"Harrumph," she snorted.

"I will spank your bottom if you don't settle down, Little girl."

The look on his face told her he wasn't joking. With a last big sigh of protest, she stopped struggling.

"Kade and the guys are home. They met with the president of the Devil's Jesters. He wasn't happy to hear from Kade. Our guys were the second set of visitors to their compound tonight."

"Who was the first?" she asked curiously.

"The police. Several people called when they witnessed the group harassing you."

"Good for them," Elizabeth announced, sitting up straighter. She hadn't been all alone. There had been people trying to help her.

"The police also arrived at the Shadowridge compound right after we left. They want to talk to you tomorrow."

"I'll stop by the station."

"We'll stop by the station—together," he corrected her.

"I don't need you to help me with this," she stated firmly. "I interact with the police frequently. It's part of my professional life. I won't have you give them the impression I'm weak."

"If you hadn't been through so much tonight, Little girl, you'd be standing in the corner now with your pants down."

Indignation struck her and her spine stiffened. She loved submitting to him in their personal time, but he was just going to have to learn that she could handle most things on her own. She hadn't put up with a husband who didn't respect how hard she worked to chisel out a space of her own as a lawyer. Elizabeth knew she was an independent, capable woman. She'd make his game backfire on him.

Dropping a few more crackers in her mouth, she stood to walk nonchalantly to the corner and pulled her blouse out of her slacks. With a few deft moves, she unfastened her waistband and pushed her slacks and panties down to the floor.

She looked over her shoulder at Talon and sneered, "This looks pretty stupid, doesn't it? I could stand here all night long."

Her bravado deserted her when he stood up to stalk forward. She turned around quickly to face the corner. He stopped just behind her.

"It appears you're asking for a time out so you can think through your choices," he growled from behind her.

"Perhaps you need a hearing test. This is totally not effective in any way. I'm not going to do what you want just because my b-u-t-t is on display," she blurted and wished she hadn't said a word when he chuckled after she spelled the word out.

"I was wrong. For a sassy Little, there is a special thinking stick for her to hold onto." Talon turned on the heel of his worn motorcycle boots and walked away.

A thinking stick? What the hell is that?

Before she could decide and act on the impulse to flee so she didn't find out, Elizabeth heard his footsteps returning.

Thump. Thump. Thump.

The boots stopped behind her. He lifted the hem of her blouse up and tucked it in the neckline. That hand pressed her forward, pushing her now fully exposed butt toward him. Without explaining, her Daddy separated her buttocks and pushed a well-lubricated plug into her bottom. In the corner, she couldn't escape.

When she reached back to pull it out, he quickly gathered her hands in front of her and wrapped them together with a fur lined restraint. Elizabeth looked up as he lifted her hands over her head. Her jaw dropped when she spotted a hook fixed into the wall above her head.

Seeing the flaw in his plan, she started to turn in a circle. She heard the thump and felt the vibration that shook the plug inside her. Instant heat flooded her body. She tried again and froze, biting her lip. What had he said? A thinking stick?

She looked over her shoulder to see what looked like a thick wooden rod emerging from her bottom. "Take that out!" Experimenting, she quickly confirmed if she turned, it would strike the wall, reverberating through her bottom.

"Not going to happen until you stop reacting and start talking to me. What's going on, Little girl?"

"Nothing. I could stand here all night," popped out of her mouth.

"Good. I don't think you're done thinking."

She peeked back over her shoulder to see him move two wooden chairs from the kitchen table to occupy the space behind her on each side. Immediately, the object he called a thinking stick whacked one chair, making her knees wobble in reaction.

"You let me know when you cool off enough to not think the worst of me and I'll finish telling you what Kade said," Talon told her in an even tone.

After a scrape on the floor, silence filled the house.

What was he doing?

Elizabeth started to turn around but a vibration on the plug filling her bottom made her stop. Something had tapped the long shaft of the thinking stick extending behind her. She tried just turning her head, but a new vibration made her stop.

"Think, Little girl. That's what the thinking stick is for."

"I don't like this," she wailed.

"Only you have the power to end this. I'm just going to sit here and tap on the thinking stick in your bottom every few minutes to remind you what you're supposed to do while you're in the corner."

"This isn't fair. I just had a scary encounter..."

Talon interrupted. "The police need to know what happened. I will be there only to explain what happened behind the scenes while you were driving."

He tapped the thinking stick again. "You may be interested in what happened at the Jester's compound."

"What happened?"

"After you finish thinking," Talon assured her and tapped the rod again.

"This is so unfair. I don't even know what I'm supposed to be thinking about," she hissed.

"How about why you're lashing out at your Daddy? Or why you needed to challenge me? Do you not think I'm your Daddy anymore? Do you need someone else? There's something going on in your mind that you're not sharing with me."

She could hear the tight rein he held on his emotions. It was killing him to ask her these questions. Hearing them out loud from him made her sick as well. Tears spilled from her eyes. Elizabeth tried to conceal them, but her breath hitched, revealing her sobs.

Immediately, everything stopped. He removed the plug and released her from the elevated hook in seconds. Gathering her onto his lap, Talon rocked her gently as he used his shirt to wipe her tears away.

"Talk to me."

"My ex-husband didn't think much of me in any way. He interfered with so many things, making it look like I was incapable of taking care of everyday things as well as my job tasks. I almost lost my position after I took him to the end of the year holiday party, and he regaled the senior partners with stories that made me look like an idiot and him the superstar."

"That sucks, Buttercup. I'm sorry. Someone obviously didn't fall for his bravado."

"There were two women partners and one man who I'd worked with on cases. They stood up for me. I was under extreme scrutiny. My divorce actually was a boon. The others realized that he was obviously not a supportive partner."

"Lawyers are pretty perceptive, I would assume."

"We definitely learn human behavior and motivation," Elizabeth agreed. "When you said I couldn't go to the police station by myself, all that stuff came back up."

"Do you think your ex-husband and I are similar?"

"Oh, good heavens, no! You're about as different from each other as possible," she assured him.

"I'd hope so. You scared me tonight, Little girl. First with the Jesters and then with your anger toward me," he told her with a very serious expression.

"I'm sorry." Tears welled again in her eyes.

"This was a very difficult day. You worked a long shift at work, dealing with things and people I can't imagine. You had some assholes chasing you down."

"This ranks in the top five of my worst days ever," she admitted.

"I'd hate to see what the other four are," he commented, and Elizabeth just shook her head. She didn't even want to think about anything else negative.

"Let's see if we can make the evening end nicely. It's past your bedtime. How about a warm shower with Daddy and a bedtime story?"

She lifted her eyebrows in a silent question before asking, "Does bedtime story mean something else?"

"No, Little girl. Bedtime story means I read you a book and you go to sleep."

"Is it going to be boring?" she asked.

"Of course not. Now up." He quickly removed her panties and slacks so she wouldn't trip as he said, "Let me put the soup away. Would you like to take some for your lunch tomorrow?"

She started to say an enthusiastic yes, but reality dawned on her. Elizabeth knew she'd never be near the refrigerator in her office or a microwave to heat it up. "No. It would be too hard to eat."

"How about cheese and some oyster crackers?"

"I'd love that," she confessed.

"Go get two plastic bags from that drawer and put crackers in one. Take all you want. I can pick up more."

Happy to help, Elizabeth stood, tugged her shirt down over her bare hips, and followed his directions. With a bag filled with the tasty oyster crackers, she wondered what cheese he wanted her to take.

As if reading her mind, Talon moved to the refrigerator and pulled out a package of cheddar cheese cubes and a few sticks of mozzarella string cheese. "These will do fine without refrigeration during the day. Take whatever you like or a combination."

With the treats stored in the fridge overnight, Talon finished in the kitchen quickly. He draped her clothing over his shoulder before wrapping his arm around her waist to guide her out of the kitchen and family room area. Turning off the lights as they passed, Talon double checked that the doors were locked.

"Is it safe here?" she blurted.

"It's safe, Buttercup. No one is going to harm you here."

"That thinking stick was…" Her voice died out as she tried to think of what to say about it.

"Effective? I thought it might be. We'll use that again with a wider plug."

"Wider? That's not necessary," she protested as they walked into the master bedroom. Elizabeth smiled automatically at the sight of Puff and Borscht tucked into bed.

"To keep your thoughts corralled to that moment in time— it's important. Thank goodness, one tip comes off and can be replaced by another. I picked it up a few years ago in preparation."

"For finding a Little?" she asked.

"For finding you," he corrected her gently as he pulled her close to take off the rest of her clothing.

Soon, he had washed all her troubles down the shower drain. Tucked into bed, Elizabeth had rolled as close as possible to her Daddy, snuggling against him as he lounged against the pillows to open a colorful book. All the struggles of the day seemed to disappear as he read in his deep voice. Puff especially loved the story because it was about flying in the sky. At least, her last thoughts were about the pretty clouds drawn in the illustrations.

CHAPTER
THIRTEEN

Elizabeth parked in a different lot the next day at the courthouse. It wasn't as convenient, but she couldn't bring herself to park in the same one where the men had threatened her. Talon had tried to convince her that she should let him drop her off at the front door and come pick her up when she was finished for the day, but she needed to be independent. She'd lied just a bit by telling him she'd be working in her office most of the day.

Now looking over her shoulder every two minutes, she wished she'd taken him up on his offer. Shaking herself mentally, Elizabeth pushed her emotions to the side and focused her energy into being prepared for that day in court. By the time she greeted her client, she felt better prepared to face the day's challenges.

Walking from the first case to hurry to her second, she took another glance when something caught her eye in a darkened doorway. Had that been a motorcycle vest? Talon wasn't checking up on her, was he?

Elizabeth stepped into the next side passageway and called him. She listened carefully to see if anyone's phone rang around her but didn't hear anything.

"Is everything okay, Buttercup?"

"Where are you?"

"I'm at the compound, working on a repair. Do you need me?" he asked.

"You didn't send any Guardians to spy on me, did you?"

"I don't like that tone or your implication I would do anything behind your back, but I'll answer your question. No. I didn't send anyone to watch over you. Do you see one of the Shadowridge Guardians at your office?"

"I'm at the courthouse now."

"Hmmm," he hummed. "And you're seeing one of our guys there?"

"Well, no. I thought I saw a leather motorcycle vest here in one of the side hallways, but I must be mistaken."

"There aren't any Shadowridge Guardians at the courthouse as far as I know. Did you recognize our logo?" he asked.

She loved that he didn't discount what she was still sure she had seen. He just asked questions to gather information. "I didn't see the back. I really didn't see much. Something caught my eye and I jumped to the conclusion that you'd sent someone to watch over me."

"I wouldn't hide that if I had. I'd be right by your side. Let me check to see if any of our regular guys are missing from the shop and I'll text you if I find out anyone was there for a personal reason. Do you want to me to come make sure everything is okay?"

"No, of course not. I must still be jumpy from last night," she admitted.

"Not working in your office today?"

"I've been here all morning. Sorry. I didn't want you to worry."

"We'll deal with your lie later. Right now, I want you to be safe. When you're close to wrapping up for the day, send me a text. I'll meet you at the front door and escort you to your car," he instructed.

"You don't have to do that," she protested, hoping he wouldn't allow her to change his mind.

"Text me if you value sitting any time in the near future," Talon warned with steel in his voice.

She looked around to make sure she was alone before answering, "Yes, Daddy."

"Good girl."

He hung up to check if any members were at the courthouse today. Elizabeth knew he wouldn't text back. She was either totally mistaken or one of the Devil's Jesters was here. Controlling her body's automatic reaction to move as the cold shiver ran down her back, Elizabeth straightened her back and walked toward her next courtroom.

Scanning the crowd subtly as she walked, Elizabeth nodded to acquaintances and the security staff. She didn't see anyone who didn't need to be there. Feeling the tension ebb from her shoulders, Elizabeth turned into the courtroom.

"There's the bitch," a familiar voice growled.

"Bailiff," Elizabeth called as she came to an abrupt stop a short distance away from the group of five bikers.

"Oh, right. Call for the jailer before you even know why we're here," Vengeance announced.

"When you greet me with foul language after you chased me down last night, I don't expect that you're here to bring me flowers," she said, forcefully keeping her tone even and flat.

"Flowers are not for ball-breaking bitches," he growled.

"Ms. Sinclair, are these men bothering you?" the bailiff asked as he rushed forward.

"For some reason, these men felt the need to call me names and stop my progress into the courtroom," Elizabeth said without emotion in her voice. She'd gone toe to toe with some people accused of horrible crimes. These guys weren't going to rattle her—even if they had chased her home.

"You'll have to leave," the bailiff ordered, pointing toward the door.

"These are witnesses for the prosecution," the opposing counsel said, rushing forward to join the conversation.

"All five of them?" Elizabeth asked with a raised eyebrow.

"Just me," Vengeance stated before adding, "They're my emotional support bikers."

The laughter from the others did not make Elizabeth or the bailiff smile.

"The others will need to leave if they can't sit down and shut up," the bailiff announced. "The judge will not tolerate any form of intimidation."

"I'd suggest you get your witness pool under control," Elizabeth told the prosecuting attorney before turning and waiting for the bikers to shift out of her way. It took several seconds for them to move.

She settled her things on the table provided for the defense and opened her briefcase to pull out a pad of paper and some documents. As the bailiff walked by to retake his position at the judge's door, Elizabeth told him, "I'd like to talk to the judge before we get started this morning."

"I'll pass along the message," he told her. "Your client is on her way."

"Thank you."

In a few moments, a frazzled-looking woman in an orange jumpsuit was brought into the courtroom. Elizabeth smiled at her as she walked to the table. "Good morning, Edith. Are you ready to start getting your life back?"

"Do they have to be here?" the woman asked, glancing over her shoulder at the leather-vested men.

"This is an open proceeding. As long as they don't create a disturbance, anyone can be here. I take it they're here to intimidate you?"

"Oh, yeah. They all want to kill me."

"Well, they're not going to touch you," Elizabeth said.

"Ms. Sinclair, the judge is ready to meet with you," the bailiff said.

The prosecuting attorney stood immediately, and Elizabeth nodded. "You're going to want to hear this."

Walking out of the courthouse at the end of the day, Elizabeth couldn't prevent the smile that curved her lips. Talon waited on the top step for her. His bike stood at the curb in a cluster of others from the Shadowridge Guardians.

"Hey, Elizabeth. We need to get you better friends," he said, straightening at the sight of the Devil's Jesters who followed her out the door. "Get behind me."

"Oh, they're not friends. For some reason, they want to shadow me. I think they're considering going to jail and needing a defense attorney," Elizabeth said with a look over her shoulder.

"Behind me, Elizabeth," he repeated as he kept his eyes on the bikers.

Elizabeth followed his directions and noted the rest of the Shadowridge Guardians stalking forward.

"Looks like he has a trained bitch," Vengeance joked.

"Seems to me there's only one bitch here." Talon's eyes stared at the large man before them.

"Talon. It's okay," Elizabeth urged. She didn't want to see a fight. Talon was densely muscled, but Vengeance towered over him by several inches and a bunch of padding.

"Go down to the bikes, Elizabeth," Steele growled as he took a position just to the left of Talon. The others clustered loosely behind them.

"Oh, it looks like you've got some buddies. Too afraid to take me on yourself, huh?"

"I'm not afraid of a piece of shit," Talon said with a dismissive tone.

It took Vengeance a full second to realize Talon was talking about him. The large man swung a fist at his target's face with amazing speed. Talon, however, was quicker.

Talon dodged faster than she'd ever seen a man move. His response to the attack was almost a blur as his fist struck Vengeance in the center of his chest, knocking the air from his lungs. Instantly, Vengeance rocked forward with his mouth open, struggling to breathe. Talon drove his thigh into the jerk's face, driving him back onto his heels.

His club members advanced but stopped as the Shadowridge Guardians stepped forward to back up Talon.

"You don't want to start this war because we will finish it," Steele told them bluntly. "No one harms those under our protection. Make no mistake that Elizabeth Sinclair is now one of us."

"Going to let the big dog fight your battles, Talon?" Vengeance taunted despite being obviously short of breath.

"Take another swing at me and find out," Talon suggested.

"Uh, Vengeance," one the Devil's Jesters said, holding onto his arm as the large man pulled it back.

When the aggressor turned his focus to his brother, the biker nodded at the security man at the entrance looking their way. "It's time to leave."

"We'll see you later," Vengeance swore as he allowed his club members to haul him away.

"Are you okay, Ms. Sinclair?" the security guard called as he walked toward the group.

"I'm fine. You may wish to alert the staff that the Devil's Jesters should be monitored when they're around the courthouse," Elizabeth called, walking forward from her safe position by the bikes.

"Got it. Watch out for motorcycle gangs," the uniformed man generalized.

"No. Not all guys in motorcycle clubs. The Devil's Jesters. They're easy to spot. They have a red jester head on their vests," Elizabeth corrected him.

"These guys are okay?" he asked, looking at the group of powerful men around her.

"These guys saved me twice," Elizabeth pointed out.

"Got it. Keep a look out for the Jesters, not all motorcycle guys in general."

"Thank you, Stanley," Elizabeth said as more guards ran from various directions to back up the security man.

"You're welcome, Ms. Sinclair," he said before turning to wave off the guys who immediately misread the Guardians' intent. "These are the good guys. Come over here and I'll share what we need to watch for."

"Come on, Little girl. I'll walk you to your car," Talon said, wrapping his arm around Elizabeth's waist.

"It's over there in the overflow parking lot," she said, pointing.

As they walked, Talon casually said, "You got here late and without anything on your calendar and had to park in overflow?"

"I'm in trouble, aren't I?"

"Oh, yeah."

They walked silently for several yards before she asked, "Is your hand okay?"

Talon looked at her in surprise. "Yes. Why?"

"You hit that guy."

"That was a love tap. I'm fine."

"I don't want a love tap then," she muttered.

"No, Buttercup. This spanking won't be a tap."

She shivered in reaction to his words and tried to pretend her body didn't race to full-arousal alert. It was going to be a long drive home.

CHAPTER
FOURTEEN

"Talon, I think my bottom is on fire!" Elizabeth called from the corner.

"Daddy, I think my bottom is on fire," he corrected in an even tone.

"Daddy, I think my bottom is on fire," she parroted, adding a sniff of unhappiness that made him smile.

"There are no active flames, Buttercup, but your cute butt is red and ouchy. When your time in the naughty corner is up, I'll spread some lotion on your skin to help you feel better before we go to dinner," Talon reassured her.

"Can I eat in here? I think someone might have overheard me."

"No, Little girl. You'll eat in the common room with everyone so you can thank them for coming to your rescue this afternoon."

"But…"

"No buts. You misbehaved. You accepted your punishment, and everything is forgiven. No one will look at you differently."

"Can I take Puff and Borscht?" she asked, hugging her companions he'd allowed her to hold during her punishment.

"Yes. I don't think they're ready to let you out of their sights."

"How much longer?" she whined.

"Three minutes if you're quiet and think about how you could have handled this better."

"Am I going to have to tell you?" she questioned.

"Four minutes now and yes."

Her snort made him smile. She was absolute perfection. The Little girl he'd always dreamed of finding. Someone whose ability to stand up for themselves was legendary but who chose to give their submission willingly. She would challenge him at every turn. He couldn't wait to see what her quick mind came up with next.

At four minutes precisely, he called her from the corner. Especially with his Buttercup, he needed to act exactly as he had promised. She'd quickly top him from below and Talon couldn't be a soft Daddy. His edges were as hard as his dance moves were smooth.

"Come here, Buttercup."

She flew into his arms and wrapped herself around him. Talon lifted her to sit on his lap, allowing her weight to rest on her thighs with her punished bottom free. He kissed her hair before leaning back to look at her expression. Tear streaks lined her face and had played havoc with her makeup. She looked absolutely perfect to him.

"That hurt, Daddy."

"And why did you get spanked?"

"Twenty swats for lying to Daddy, thirty for putting myself at risk, and ten removed for realizing I had a problem and calling you."

"What are you going to do differently?" Talon ignored her massive eye roll and waited for her to talk.

"I'm going to tell you the truth."

"And not put yourself in jeopardy?" he prompted.

"What could I have done? Ask you to drive me to the court-house?" she demanded.

Her tone immediately changed as he raised one eyebrow and firmly tapped her bottom. That seemed to help her think.

"Oops. I could have asked you to take me to work?"

"That would have been better."

"Okay. You're right. I screwed up and now I have a hot bottom to remind me."

She paused for a few seconds before peeking up to ask, "Can I have some lotion on my skin?"

"Yes. And I'll let you wear leggings tonight so they'll be soft on your skin," Talon told her as he lifted her back to her feet.

"Oh, you mean instead of panties," she said with a nod as he guided her into the bedroom.

"I mean instead of being bare bottomed and just wearing one of your dresses," Talon explained and stopped when Elizabeth whirled to look at him in astonishment.

"I can't go out there with all those people without panties or at least pants."

"No one there is going to notice unless you turn cartwheels," Talon pointed out.

"But I'll know," she hissed. "And you'll know."

"Exactly."

Talon wrapped his arm back around her waist and guided her into the bedroom. When she was dressed, he washed her face free of makeup and took her hand.

"Hungry?" he asked.

"Starving."

"Let's go."

"Are you sure they won't look at me strange?" she asked, nervous they had overheard her crying during her spanking.

"They're going to be concerned if you've recovered from the confrontation on the courthouse steps. They know you were punished for putting yourself at risk."

"And they would have spanked me, too?" She needed to double-check.

"If you were their Little girl, yes."

"Okay." She linked her fingers with his and warned, "I'm sitting on your lap instead of one of those mean wooden chairs."

"This time," he allowed with a warning glance.

"Oh, you won't have to spank me anymore."

"Yes, I will. When you find out you have an appointment with Doc on Saturday for a check-up."

"Doc? He isn't a real doctor."

Talon knew she wasn't being derogatory. She liked Doc a lot and knew the other girls had discussed his care with her during their "private" time in the fort. Elizabeth was simply back pedaling.

"He's something even better. He knows medicine and cares about you. And he's aware how Little girls don't take care of themselves and how their Daddies can help them."

"We'll talk about it on the weekend," she suggested.

"We can talk all you want," he answered in a tone that told her nothing was going to change as they walked out the door.

The aroma of taco night made them both speed up. Food would distract his Little girl for a short time. Talon knew there would be an emergency meeting of the Littles to discuss being treated by Doc.

"Can I ask you guys something?" Elizabeth whispered as she leaned into the gathering of Littles.

"Do we need to go to the library?" Remi suggested in an equally quiet tone.

"Yes, please." Elizabeth nodded.

She looked over her shoulder to meet Talon's eyes and pantomimed opening a book before pointing to the small room next to the kitchen. After he nodded his permission, she followed the other girls.

"Daddy said I have an appointment with Doc for a check-up

on Sunday," she whispered furiously. "I tried to get out of it, but I don't think that's going to be possible."

"Nope. With a red bottom or without, if your Daddy warned you, he's set on hearing from Doc what he needs to do to keep you healthy," Remi warned.

"But... Doc is Harper's Daddy."

"That doesn't matter," Ivy stated bluntly. "Doc treats all of us."

"What does Harper say about this?" Elizabeth asked, bristling.

When everyone turned to look at Harper, she blushed at being the center of attention. Stumbling over her words, she tried to explain. "My Daddy isn't going to become your Daddy or anyone else's Daddy just because he sees you naked. He sees a lot of people naked."

Realizing what she said, Harper rushed to add, "He's trained to make people feel better. He was a medic in the army for a long time. Now as a paramedic with the firefighters, he still uses his medical skills to save lives. He treats all the Shadowridge Guardians. You saw him take two of Rock's loaded tacos and pour it on a bed of lettuce at dinner tonight."

"But you're okay if he sees us naked? Daddy's going to make me get naked," Elizabeth warned.

"All the Daddies make Littles get naked in the medical room. I think it's like the law. At first it made me nervous that he'd think you all were prettier than me, but Daddy explained about the difference of seeing a Little through the eyes of her Daddy and as a medical practitioner," Harper explained.

Elizabeth stopped and thought for a minute. "That makes sense. I hadn't thought of him like two different people. Doc loves you so much. That's easy for everyone to see."

Harper smiled and nodded. "He chose me. I don't know why."

"I do. You're amazing and he knows he found the perfect Little girl to make his," Elizabeth stressed.

"Exactly," Remi chimed in.

"Yes!" Ivy agreed and everyone else nodded.

Harper smiled and wrapped her arms around herself. "We really are lucky to have found our Daddies. Even if Elizabeth has a sore butt."

"Don't remind me," Elizabeth joked, rubbing her bottom.

"What are you going to do about the Devil's Jesters?" Carlee asked.

"I don't know. I get the feeling something is going on. Why come to the courthouse where there's always going to be security? It doesn't make any sense," Elizabeth mused.

"You're there," Ivy pointed out.

"Yeah. That's what I'm afraid of. Why are they coming at me?"

"You need to be careful," Harper warned.

"Oh, I will be," Elizabeth promised.

CHAPTER
FIFTEEN

hank goodness it's Friday.

Elizabeth loved her job and all her commitments, but this week had been a doozy. It had also been a good week. She and Talon had dined with her parents. Seeing Talon in the one tailored suit he owned had almost made her call to cancel. Staying home to play "Find the Tattoos" was very tempting. To her surprise, they had given him a chance. Of course, Talon's charm had won them over. He'd also brought a very unique hostess gift her mother loved. Thank goodness, the pickled beets had found someone who would love them.

She'd break it to them gently that he was in a motorcycle club. In a few months.

Professionally, Elizabeth had won her cases and felt like she'd helped people. Sometimes working in the court system was frustrating. There was only room for rights and wrongs even if shades of gray should exist.

Finishing her last case at the courthouse, Elizabeth slid her papers back in her briefcase as she mentally reviewed her schedule. She had a couple of meetings back at her office and then she could head home to Talon.

"Home," she repeated to herself.

It had been a long time since she'd actually wanted to have time off. Spending the weekend with her ex-husband had been stressful and unpleasant. Then after their divorce, the quiet had been overwhelming. Going home sounded good again now.

Smiling, she turned to leave the trial area. The grizzled face in front of her made her grab her phone.

"Don't. Actually, you can if you want. Talon should know what's going on," Vengeance said.

She knew he remained sitting to appear less threatening. His bulk would automatically put people on alert. "What's going on?"

"I'd like to hire you. Well, Slash needs to hire you."

"What? Hire me to do what?"

"Is there somewhere we could talk?" he asked as people bustled into the courtroom for the next proceeding.

"I'm not comfortable being alone with you," Elizabeth said bluntly.

"I get that."

Searching his face, Elizabeth noted none of the aggressive posturing she'd seen with Vengeance each time she'd met him before. She wasn't going to forget his bullying behavior at the farmer's market, but whatever had brought him here must be important for him to give her a peek behind the Devil's Jester persona.

She pulled up her schedule on her phone. "I have ninety minutes open this afternoon at four. Do you want to meet me in my office? Be aware, I will have others with me for protection."

"Slash will need to come," Vengeance added.

"And Slash wishes to talk to me?"

"He'll be there," Vengeance promised.

"Four o'clock promptly." Elizabeth pulled a card from her pocket with her contact information and handed it over.

Nodding, the large biker stood and tucked the card in his pocket before heading for the exit.

"Is everything okay, Ms. Sinclair?" the bailiff asked.

Aware the officer had hovered behind her during the conversation to make sure everything was okay, Elizabeth smiled and said, "Thank you for the backup. I think everything is okay. I need to make a phone call, and then could someone walk me to my car just in case?"

"Of course. I'll alert them at the front desk."

"Thank you."

Selecting Talon's number, she walked from the courtroom and leaned back against a wall.

"Trouble?"

She could hear him moving and knew he was preparing to come to her. "I'm okay. I hope you can meet me at my office at four. Slash and Vengeance have made an appointment to discuss hiring me."

"Those assholes can find another lawyer."

"You don't get to make that decision."

"Little girl..."

She interrupted him. "I know you're concerned. I am, too. My office staff will be on alert and I'm inviting you to be there. This is my job."

"I don't like this."

Elizabeth could feel the tension in his words. "I know."

"I'll be there at three."

"You don't need to come scare people in my office," she said with a smile, understanding he'd backed away from his complete refusal for her to see them. "And don't bring the Shadowridge Guardians. I don't want everyone on edge and ready to explode."

She could hear him thinking as the silence stretched between them.

Finally, he said, "I'll be there alone, but everyone will be on alert."

"And at least five miles away from my office."

"You're demanding a lot, Little girl. I don't like it."

"I know."

"I'll be there at three," he stated firmly.

"I look forward to seeing you."

Clicking off the call, Elizabeth smiled at her phone. That had gone better than she expected.

Talon's three o'clock actually started at two fifteen, but Elizabeth didn't do anything more than smile at him as she walked through the reception area to pick up the woman who was her two thirty appointment. Her staff was used to a wide variety of people visiting her. Most of the toughest characters were already in jail and she visited them there.

She continued with her day and even had a few minutes to work on paperwork before a message came through that her four o'clock appointment had arrived. After taking one last sip of coffee to bolster herself, Elizabeth headed for the lobby. Talon sat on one side of the arranged chairs while Slash and Vengeance occupied the other.

"Come in, gentlemen," she invited with a wave toward her office.

As she sat behind her desk, Talon leaned against the wall near where the two chairs for her guests sat. "This is out of the norm for a meeting, but given the events leading up to the appointment, it seems appropriate. Slash, I understand this meeting is for you."

"Vengeance dragged me here," the Devil's Jesters' president growled.

"And you agree to have Vengeance and Talon here during our conversation?" Elizabeth asked pointedly.

"Yes," he said through gritted teeth.

"Tell me what's going on and I'll let you know whether or

not I think I can help you," Elizabeth requested, dragging a pad in front of her and picking up a pen to make notes.

"My old lady died six months ago. Her parents are trying to take our kids."

"Your old lady as in your girlfriend?" Elizabeth tried to unravel what he was saying.

"We weren't married but had been together for eleven years. She got sick and refused to go to the doctor. By the time I got her there, the doctors said there was nothing left to do. She was gone fast," Slash reported. His voice was mechanical as if he were forcing himself to keep any emotion at bay.

"I'm sorry. Did you live together?"

"Yes."

"With the children?"

"Yes. I have a small home in Lexington."

"Thank you. And her parents are now seeking custody of the children?"

"Yes. They state I am not a good influence on their lives and can't provide a stable homelife." Slash's face took on a shade of red and Elizabeth knew he was trying to control his temper as he recited words he'd obviously memorized in anger.

"Do you have a criminal record?" she asked.

"None after eighteen."

"Juvenile records usually remain sealed. No charges currently pending?" Elizabeth continued to gather background.

"No."

"So, they're alleging you're not a good parent because you are a Devil's Jester?"

"Yes."

"And you plan to continue to be a Devil's Jester?" Elizabeth verified.

"I won't lose my children," Slash said definitively.

"Tell me about her parents. What are their names? Are they retired? What did they do?"

"Alena Mitchell was a truck driver and Jack Hambly owns a trucking company."

"They aren't married?"

"No. They don't believe in marriage. At least that's what Jalena told me."

"What was Jalena's last name?"

"Mitchell. Jalena lived most of the time with her grand-mother because her mom was on the road, driving loads cross country," Slash shared.

"And Jack Hambly? How involved was her father in Jalena's life?"

"I never heard her talk about him. I don't think he was even around while Jalena was growing up."

"What do you do?" Elizabeth asked.

Slash shifted uncomfortably in his chair. Vengeance elbowed him and nodded at Elizabeth in an awkwardly encouraging man exchange.

"I design and create playground equipment."

Elizabeth heard Talon exhale in surprise and saw him lean closer. Understanding the surprised reaction, she deliberately didn't look his way.

"How old are your children? What are their names?"

"Jalinda is nine and Jerome is seven. They go to Lexington elementary school. Jalinda is in fourth grade and Jerome is in second."

"How do your work hours match your children's?"

"I flex my hours to theirs. If one is sick and can't go to school, my parents stay with them. They're both retired teachers," Slash explained.

"Do they have any reason to question the stability of your household? Are there financial concerns or difficulties with the school?"

"No. My house is paid off. I don't believe in spoiling kids, but we have everything we need. Their bellies are full and they're healthy."

"You haven't talked to a lawyer about this?" Elizabeth questioned.

"I thought they'd drop it. They've never been interested in the kids before. Or any of us. We spend holidays and free time with my folks. We always have—even when Jalena was here."

"Do you know why they're doing this?"

"I think they want the money."

"Money?" Elizabeth echoed.

"Jalena was a gambler. A good one. That's how we met. She wiped me out during a poker game and then bought me a beer to apologize."

"She had money?"

"A lot. Four hundred thousand dollars. It's in a special account at the bank for the kids' college tuition."

"And it can be accessed to pay for their upkeep?" Elizabeth guessed.

"Yes. But I'll never do that. They're smart kids. Jerome is skipping third grade next year to go on to fourth."

"Okay, I think I've got everything I need. Slash, there's no way anyone should be able to take your kids away—despite your participation in a motorcycle club—unless there is evidence the Devil's Jesters are involved in illegal activities. Can your guys stay away from anything negative for a year?"

"A year?" Vengeance echoed.

"That's probably how long this will take to go through the family court. These things move slow," Elizabeth confirmed. "This isn't my specialty. I'm a defense attorney who deals with criminal charges. You need a lawyer well versed in family law. I have the perfect suggestion for you, though."

"Someone else won't understand," Slash said, shaking his head.

"It doesn't take experience with a motorcycle group to understand a money grab. My colleague is intelligent, compassionate, and right down the hall. She's who I would hire if I needed a family lawyer. Should I call to see if she can come join our meeting?"

"She's good?" Slash asked, staring directly at Elizabeth.

"She's the best."

"Do it."

As Elizabeth found her colleague's number, Slash said, "Thank you, Elizabeth. My kids are everything to me. They're all I have left of their mother."

"Then we're going to take care of this. No scary moves from here on out. If you want to make an appointment, call and schedule one. Don't chase her down with a horde of bikers," Elizabeth warned.

Slash nodded. "It seemed like a good idea at the time to convince you."

A snort of laughter exploded from Talon at the side of the room. Vengeance and Slash turned to look at him as Elizabeth held her breath.

"Only bikers would think of recruiting a lawyer with a posse," Talon said with a smirk.

Vengeance bristled and tightened his hands into fists, immediately ready to take insult. To Elizabeth's relief, Slash put a hand on his forearm and shook his head. "He's right. It was a biker thing to do. Jump into battle first."

"Your kids are worth making a good plan," Talon suggested.

"Damn right, they are," Slash answered.

CHAPTER
SIXTEEN

L ate Friday night, Talon looked at the Guardians sitting at the table. He'd sat in on a couple of the leaders' meetings at Atlas's request when the budget was discussed. Steele had called him into the meeting this time to detail the recent events.

"The Devil's Jesters are a thorn in our side, but they're going to leave my Little girl alone," Talon reported.

"How sure are you that the Littles are safe?" Steele demanded.

"The Jesters are going to walk a tightrope for a year as Slash fights to save his kids. I don't think we'll see a lot of them," Talon suggested. "As to how safe our Littles are? I don't trust them as far as I could throw Vengeance."

"How did Elizabeth get on their radar in the first place?" Kade asked.

"There was a letter to the editor in the local newspaper detailing the heroism of a lawyer who put herself at risk to save a vendor at the farmer's market."

"Don't tell me Slash reads the local throwaway paper," Atlas scoffed.

"Vengeance does," Talon said.

Steele simply shook his head. "We'll keep an eye on them. Kade, I'm going to leave that to you."

"Got it," Kade assured him.

Even if he hadn't been asked, Talon knew the Enforcer would have made this his business. Talon didn't particularly like that Slash would be around Elizabeth's office. They would need to have a very serious talk about her keeping her distance from any of the Jesters.

"I'll let the club know they don't need to be on high alert," Kade stated firmly.

"I owe you guys for protecting my Little girl," Talon said.

"She's yours. That makes her one of ours," Storm commented.

"I'm just waiting for her to sue you for being a smart ass," Rock said with an almost straight face.

"Thank goodness, she likes me better than you bastards," Talon rebutted. "It must be my dance moves."

When the laughter died out at Talon's spontaneous chair dancing, Steele said, "We do have another issue we need to discuss."

All eyes focused on Steele as he referred to the paperwork in front of him. "Atlas and Talon have reviewed the accounts. The club's funds are still low after Silver but rebounding."

Steele paused as names were offered to describe their former treasurer. None of them were flattering.

"Old pebble balls?" Talon suggested, leaning in to enjoy the fun.

"Continuing," Steele drew them back together. "We are above water now. The repair shop is running at capacity. We may need more bays to deal with all the weekend riders."

"And more Guardians?" Atlas suggested.

"Yes. Just because a guy is good with a wrench doesn't get them into the Shadowridge Guardians," Kade pointed out.

"We've had more women bringing bikes in. Maybe we need a lady on staff," Doc suggested.

"That's not a bad idea," Steele agreed. "Let's start advertising for staff. Who knows what will straggle in? What do you think of the prospects?"

Talon sat back and listened to the discussion of their current prospects and who might have earned their way into the Guardians. The discussion was brutal and intense. No one wanted the wrong guy to make it into the MC. They'd already seen what happened when someone went rogue.

"Ink has my vote," he tossed into the conversation.

"Agreed. What do you think of the others?" Kade asked, looking around the room. "I have a few more who've asked about being part of the club."

Curled up on the couch with a big bowl of popcorn, Elizabeth tried to wrap her mind around the idea that the problem with the Jesters was settled. Only now did she realize how much stress she'd carried around as she had looked over her shoulder constantly. Trying to balance work, her new relationship with Talon, and a threat to her personal safety had swamped her emotions.

A tear ran down her face and was quickly followed by another. She wiped them away, trying not to disturb anyone else, but once the torrent started, Elizabeth couldn't stop. A heart-deep sob tore from her mouth, drawing attention.

"Elizabeth? Are you okay?" Remi asked.

"I'm… I'm fine." She finally pushed the words past her lips. Feeling her nose start to run, Elizabeth panicked and tried to sit up to find her napkin.

In a flurry of puffy whiteness, popcorn flew all over Elizabeth, the couch, and the floor. With her nose running, popcorn everywhere, and tears pouring from her eyes, she slumped against the back of the couch in utter despair. Ivy handed her a tissue before scooping the popcorn off the couch onto the floor to make a spot for herself. She wrapped her arms around Elizabeth's heaving shoulders.

"Go get Talon. She needs her Daddy," Ivy urged the others.

Harper flew across the room.

"Buttercup?" Talon knelt in front of her a few seconds later.

She launched herself forward to press as close as possible to her Daddy as he pulled her tight. Elizabeth knew Ivy would understand her need to be near Talon. Wrapping her arms around his neck, she clung to him as tears continued to pour down her cheeks.

"Little girl, you're scaring me. Are you hurt?" Talon asked urgently as his hands searched over her body.

"I just can't... can't stop... crying." She tried to explain but was having trouble getting the words out of her mouth.

Using the bottom of his worn-soft, cotton shirt, he wiped off her face. "Oh, baby. Maybe we should have Doc check you over tonight," he suggested.

Elizabeth could see the concern etched on his face. She tried to pull herself together but just couldn't. "Nooo!" she wailed.

She felt a cool hand on her forehead and looked to see Doc next to them. Her arms tightened around her Daddy. Elizabeth wasn't letting him go.

Doc quietly took her pulse. "You are so upset, Little girl. Did everything just become too much?" he asked.

"Yes."

"Is she okay?" Talon asked, rocking her in his arms.

"She's just where she needs to be. A bit of Daddy time and Elizabeth will be ready to take on anything," Doc assured them both.

"I'd like that, too," Talon said, brushing the hair from her face. "Come on, Little girl. I need you to myself."

Standing, he scooped her off the couch and carried her through the crowd that had gathered, scattering popcorn like rose petals in their wake. Elizabeth peeked away from his shoulder to see the big, tough bikers, who had defended her without a second's hesitation, watching with worried expressions. She should have been embarrassed but wasn't.

With a sigh of relief, she laid her head on Talon's shoulder and closed her eyes. Her Daddy had her.

At their apartment, he opened the door and stalked inside, softly closing the door behind them. Shifting her slightly, he sat down in his overstuffed recliner. Talon stroked over her hair as he rocked the chair slowly.

"I love you, Elizabeth Marie Sinclair."

The words sizzled into her brain. Another man had fooled her with that phrase, but this time, they felt real and truthful. She couldn't compare Talon with anyone else. He'd always been straightforward with her. She knew he wasn't telling her he loved her to make her feel better. He didn't blow smoke up anyone's ass.

Elizabeth pressed her hand to his heart and felt the powerful muscle beat steadily under her palm. Her world seemed to solidify around her. A memory of their brunch together popped into her mind. Before they'd gone to eat, he'd shown her how much pleasure and fun she'd missed out on in life. He'd simply turned her life upside down. Or was it right side up?

"Do you love me more than bacon?" she whispered, remembering their conversation about taking risks and enjoying the rewards.

"Definitely more than bacon, Buttercup." He raised one hand up to eye level. "Here's how much I love bacon. And this is how much I love you."

She watched his hand rise to way over their heads. "I love you more than bacon, too," she whispered. "I'm sorry I got so upset."

"It was about time for you to melt down. Since we've met, you've scurried from one adrenaline rush to another. All with poise and grace. I don't know how you've done it."

"That's what I'm supposed to do. You know—as a lawyer."

"You're a damn fine lawyer. The best one I've ever met."

"How many lawyers do you know?"

"There's you... really, there's just you. I don't care about anyone else."

She stared at him for several long seconds as thoughts whirled in her head. The calmness of his reaction to her meltdown reassured her. Elizabeth felt like she could actually be a real person with Talon. That was a pretty unbelievable thought. Slowly, she felt everything click back into place and smiled at him.

"Better?"

"Yes, thank you."

Elizabeth rubbed her eyes and smoothed her hair, trying to put herself back into some kind of order. Leaning forward, she pressed her mouth against Talon's. The kiss was sweet and light until he cradled her head in one hand to hold her steady as he deepened the exchange. Her body flared with need. Elizabeth pushed a hand against his chest to shift back and he immediately released her.

"You okay, Buttercup?"

"No. I need you to make me scream."

"Spanking or orgasm?"

"Orgasm. Multiple." She went for broke.

Talon's smile told her he was very willing and able to make that request come true. He pulled her soft top over her head and tossed it aside, stopping briefly to pluck a piece of popcorn out of her hair. Talon popped it into his mouth as he admired her form.

Daringly, Elizabeth locked her gaze with his before running her hands over his broad shoulders and down his arms to where they rested at her waist. She stroked up her torso to cradle her breasts in her hands, kneading them temptingly. The sensation made her eyelids lower slightly, but she struggled to keep her gaze on her Daddy's face. The heat etched into his expression made her squirm.

He groaned, and she realized her body moved against his rapidly hardening cock. Elizabeth did it again—just because. His hands tightened around her hips, holding her in place.

To tempt him further, Elizabeth tugged her nipples, making herself moan in delight.

"Little girls who tease their Daddies get more than they anticipate," Talon growled.

"I'm counting on that."

Elizabeth released her breasts to shift her hands to the bottom of his T-shirt. She allowed her fingers to brush over the erection tenting his jeans as if by accident. When he froze, she grabbed the bottom of his shirt and tugged it upward. "Help me, Daddy."

Talon lifted one arm to reach over his shoulder in an amazing display of muscles to yank the material over his head. Throwing it away, he never took his gaze off her. "You're wearing too many clothes. Let's take care of that problem."

Without an ounce of visible effort or strain, Talon picked her up and stood her in front of him. He leaned forward to trap one nipple in his mouth and swirled his tongue around the taut peak as he stripped her leggings and panties down her legs. Releasing his target with an audible pop, he commanded, "Lift your left leg. Now your right," as he tugged the garments over her feet.

When she started to move back onto his lap, Talon stopped her with a hand up in front of her. "Touch yourself for Daddy."

"What?" she squeaked.

"Touch yourself," he repeated as he unbuttoned his jeans.

Torn between watching his expression and his hands, Elizabeth's gaze darted up and down—getting distracted frequently by his chiseled torso.

"Elizabeth." He reminded her of the task he had given her.

"Oh!" Cupping her breasts once again, she caressed her body, unable to feel self-conscious because of the heat in his gaze. Elizabeth could see how turned on he was as his jeans burst open when he drew the zipper carefully downward.

Feeling powerful, Elizabeth stroked one hand down her abdomen. She rubbed lightly over the mound between her legs as he stood slightly to push his jeans and boxers over his hips. His gaze frozen on her, he dropped back to the seat to pull the garments off.

"Damn boots," he cursed when everything became snagged.

"I can help," Elizabeth volunteered and tried to pull one off for him.

"Turn around and straddle my leg, Little girl," he ordered. "Grab the boot and pull."

Leaning over to snare the footwear, Elizabeth peeked over her shoulder to see her Daddy looking squarely at her bottom. She bit her lower lip at the arousal on his face. Pulling quickly, the boot came off with a pop.

She pushed the material off over his ankle, freeing his leg before shifting to the other side. This time, she had trouble tugging it off. Elizabeth stood up as she felt his stocking foot press against her bottom.

"I'm just helping you, Buttercup. That boot's a bit tight," he assured her.

Taking his word for it, she leaned over again to pull. His foot pressed into her ass, increasing the pressure on the boot to give. That was all it took. Elizabeth stumbled forward with the empty boot in her hands. She dropped it to the floor with a clunk as she regained her balance.

"Good girl," he complimented as he removed the last of his clothing.

She smiled and raised her arms in triumph. When his gaze focused on her bouncing breasts, she chose to channel her inner vamp. It wasn't embarrassing when it had such a marked effect on him.

Elizabeth lifted a hand to twirl a lock of hair around as she looked over his body. All hard angles, she loved the incredible strength that showed in each inch of his body. As her gaze settled on his thick erection, she licked her lips.

"You are going to kill me, Little girl. Let me grab a condom."

"No condoms, Daddy."

"You're protected?" he asked, gripping the arms of the chair as if holding himself back.

She nodded and whispered, "Daddy? Make me come."

With a roar, Talon jumped up from the chair and wrapped his arms around her, carrying her toward the wall.

"Wrap your legs around my waist," he ordered as he pressed her against the hard surface. "There's no way we're making it to a bed for the first time."

Following his instructions, she echoed, "The first time?"

"I hope you don't have to walk far tomorrow," he growled as he lifted her hips slightly to align their bodies.

He flexed his hips, and she inhaled quickly as the broad head of his cock pressed into her entrance. She was so wet, allowing him to slide several inches inside in one stroke. Talon leaned forward to kiss her lips hard. Lifting his head a scant few inches, he praised her, "That's it, Buttercup. Take my cock. You feel so good around me."

She nodded. "More, Daddy."

Pushing rapidly into her, Talon forced her body to relax around him until their bodies met together. The stretch and slight burn fueled her arousal. She loved knowing how much he craved being inside her. Elizabeth could feel her body quivering around his thickness.

"Move, damn it," she ordered, knowing he was waiting for her to adjust to his invasion.

Slamming his mouth over hers, Talon withdrew and thrust back inside strongly. His mouth made love to hers, seducing her with searing kisses that took her breath away. She quickly lost herself in the sensations buffeting her body, seeking only to return the pleasure he lavished on her with caresses and temptations of her own.

Their skin dampened with sweat as their bodies strained together. His hands cupped her bottom as his pelvis held her trapped against the wall. The small rubbing thrust pressed fully on her clit, thrilling her. Elizabeth looped one arm around his neck to help support her weight, but Talon showed no signs of struggling to hold her in place. His expression held only fierce desire and need.

"There," Elizabeth cried out when his stroke made her squirm with excitement. She slid her hands to his shoulders, gripping him tightly as she held her breath. A few seconds later, she wailed as the climax shook her body.

Talon gentled his motions, extending her pleasure rather than intensifying it too much. Elizabeth kissed him, pouring all her emotions into the exchange. His heated response made the heat inside her rekindle.

Tearing his mouth from hers, Talon warned, "Hold on." A fraction of a second later, he stepped back from the wall.

With a squeak of surprise, she tightened her arms around his neck and then moaned as he walked to the small breakfast table. Each step sent sensations through her. Carefully, he set her bottom on the edge of cold wood, making her shiver. *A man who'll take me on the kitchen table?*

Just as that thought zinged into her brain, Talon withdrew and thrust back inside in one stimulating move, making them both groan with delight. She'd never imagined sex could be this good. Elizabeth stroked her hands over his chest, tracing those tattoos decorating his chest and arms.

Now with his hands free, Talon could caress her body as he moved inside her. Wiggling with pleasure, she returned his thrilling touches with ones of her own, tightening her pelvic muscles to squeeze him.

With a wicked look in his eyes, Talon stroked down her body to tease her clit. She tried to resist, but he knew exactly how to push her control to the breaking point. With a cry, Elizabeth exploded. The orgasm shook her body and clamped her channel around his thick shaft inside her.

His growl flowed over her as he poured himself inside her. She loved the feel of the warm heat coating her as Talon wrapped his arms around her. He lifted her from the table to hug her against his chest. Elizabeth rested her head on his shoulder as she tried to regain control of her breath and thundering heart.

"It was the best day ever when I found you," he told her. "I'm never letting you go, Buttercup."

"That's good because that was way better than bacon," she said, teasing him.

"I'll make you forget bacon exists next time."

"Next time?" she questioned, leaning back to look at him.

"You asked for multiple orgasms. You're not done yet. And neither am I," he said. Squeezing her tightly against his chest, Talon carried her to the bedroom.

CHAPTER
SEVENTEEN

fter breakfast and a long soak in the tub, Elizabeth was ready to curl up in bed to take a nap. Wrapped in a towel, she sat on the counter as her Daddy dried her hair. She loved the warm air and the rhythmic stroke of the brush through her tresses as she watched his handsome face concentrating on his efforts. *He is so dedicated to being a good Daddy.*

A knock on the door made her clutch the towel wrapped around her. "Who's that? Could you tell the Littles I can't play until I get dressed?"

"I'll tell them. I have a feeling it's someone else," Talon hinted as he left the bathroom to answer the door.

Who else would come to the door?

Hearing the male voice answer Talon's greeting, she remembered her appointment with Doc. She froze in place, looking around to find somewhere to hide. Foiled by Talon's return, she said, "I'm good. I don't need to see Doc today," as she hopped down from the vanity.

"This is a check-up to keep you healthy," Talon reminded her, taking her hand to lead her into the main room.

"Hi, Elizabeth. I'm here to take you and your Daddy to the medical room."

Pressing her hands to the sides of her face, she quickly addressed Doc. "Hi! Sorry to waste your time. I'm good."

"I'm glad to hear that. Let's go make sure."

Elizabeth squeaked when her Daddy picked her up in his arms and carried her out the door that Doc held open for them. It all happened so fast she didn't protest. She was more worried about running into anyone dressed only in a towel. They walked down the empty hallway to a room with Medical written on it in big letters. Doc opened the door to an already lighted room equipped with an examination table. She swallowed hard when she saw the leg supports usually used in a pelvic exam.

"Have a seat on the table. Your Daddy will help you," Doc told her.

"Oh, I meant I don't need an exam," she rushed to assure him as Talon set her on the paper-topped table.

Talon wrapped his hands around her waist to tether her in place when she wiggled to get off the crinkly surface. When she looked at her Daddy, begging him with her eyes to go back to their room, he said softly, "You will have an exam. I want you to be healthy and happy. Doc takes care of everyone here. Did you talk to the other Littles about seeing him?"

"I did. They all said they've had an exam. Harper said she knows her Daddy loves her." Leaning in, she whispered in Talon's ear, "I don't want to be naked in front of Doc."

"That's *going* to happen, Little girl. He can't make sure you're okay if he doesn't check everywhere."

Doc looped his stethoscope around his neck and told her, "Elizabeth, I've seen a lot of men and women naked over the years. Everyone comes in different shapes and sizes. I don't care what your body looks like. I only care that you are healthy."

Studying his face, she could see he was telling the truth. "I'm scared," she confessed.

"I understand that. Your Daddy is by your side, but I think

you need backup. Is your bear here? Wasn't his name Vichyssoise?"

A giggle escaped her at the thought of a stuffie with a name that fancy. "No, his name is Borscht."

"That might be easier to spell?" Doc asked, looking quizzically at her as if he wasn't sure about that fact.

"I'll get Borscht," Talon assured her. "Stay right there."

He ran down the hall and was back in a flash. Elizabeth used the time to look around and noticed Doc had several things on the counter to use. She was scooting toward the edge of the table when Talon returned and looped an arm around her waist to haul her backwards.

"Let's not have you fall off the table, Buttercup," he said as he handed her bear to her.

Elizabeth hid her face in his soft pink fur. He did make her feel better. "Thank you."

"Alright. You hug Borscht and I'll check a few things," Doc said as he grabbed a handheld device from the counter.

After checking her eyes and ears, he asked her to open her mouth and say, "Ah."

"Ahhhhhh!" Elizabeth followed directions, pulling out the word as he looked at her throat.

"Everything looks pretty good. I'm a bit worried that your eyes are slightly bloodshot. Have you had your eyes tested lately?" Doc asked.

Elizabeth nodded ruefully. "I'm supposed to wear glasses when I read a lot of documents. I forget to put them on sometimes."

"I can tell. That's a good thing for you and your Daddy to work on," Doc suggested.

"Oh, I'll do better at remembering," Elizabeth rushed to assure them both.

"Daddy will help. That's my job, right? To take care of you," Talon told her firmly.

"Pulse next," Doc warned.

She appreciated him telling her what he was doing. It made her less anxious. Elizabeth held out one hand so he could feel her pulse at her wrist.

"A bit elevated but I seem to worry people sometimes," Doc said. "I do want to check your blood pressure."

Sitting still as he wrapped a cuff around her upper arm, Elizabeth hugged Borscht with the other hand. She tried to think calm thoughts.

"High, Little girl. Has your regular doctor talked to you about some medicine?" Doc asked, pinning her in place with his observant gaze.

"Well, yes. We've talked about it. I promised to work out more and watch my salt intake."

"And did you do that?" Doc probed.

She shifted uncomfortably on the table. "No."

Talon pulled out his phone and opened a new note. "I better make a list. Glasses, exercise, salt."

"We'll recheck this every month to see if it comes down. If it doesn't in a couple months, you're going back to the doctor for a prescription. There's no shame in taking medicine. There is harm in damaging your heart when you can prevent it. I have a feeling the stress of your job and the long hours take a toll on you. Exercise and sufficient rest is probably going to help the most. There's a walking trail through the land behind the complex. A stroll after work would help you relax. I bet a bunch of Littles would like to go with you. Then, it's not really exercise, it's 'let's go look at the tadpoles in the creek' or 'there's a fawn in the woods'."

"There's a baby fawn in the woods?" she asked, instantly intrigued.

"Maybe?" Doc suggested. "Let me listen to your chest and lungs."

Talon reached forward to unfasten the towel wrapped around her.

"Daddy! No!" Elizabeth clutched his hands, holding the material in place.

"This is going to come off, Little girl. Do you want to cooperate now or with a red bottom?" Talon asked.

Not liking the stern look on his face, Elizabeth whispered, "Don't make me."

"Doc can't listen to your lungs through the thick material, Little girl. I've already learned you aren't doing everything you should to take care of yourself. He's here to help," Talon assured her.

She stared at him for several long seconds, expecting him to back down, but Talon looked steadily back at her with a resolute expression. With a sigh, Elizabeth closed her eyes and let go of his hands. She felt the material slide down her body to puddle around her waist.

"This may be cold, Little girl," Doc warned and pressed the stethoscope to her chest. He listened in several places, even under her breasts, but his touch remained professional. When he switched to her back, Elizabeth pulled the towel up to cover her chest.

"Your heart and lungs sound very healthy. Time to lie on your side," Doc directed.

Confused, Elizabeth started to follow his directions. As she shifted on the exam table, Talon unwound the towel from around her body and draped it over her side. She heard Doc pick up something from the counter behind her. Looking over her shoulder, she watched the medic offer a fairly large box to her Daddy.

"Do you need another thermometer? This is what I recommend for Little girls."

"Yes. I took the one I had here to Elizabeth's apartment," Talon told him as he accepted the item.

"Use whatever lubricant you prefer," Doc told him.

"Lubricant?" Elizabeth echoed.

Doc patted her hip. She watched him maneuver gloves onto

his oversized hands and then squeeze a generous amount of a thick substance from a large tube onto his fingertip. When he lifted the towel over her bottom, Elizabeth squealed and tried to roll back over.

"None of that, Little girl," Talon said, firmly pressing his hand against her hip before pulling her top knee across her body to rest on the edge of the table, tethering Elizabeth in place on her side.

Without delaying, Doc spread her buttocks and rubbed lubricant around her small rosette. He pushed a finger into her bottom and moved it around to coat the walls of her tight channel with the slippery mixture.

"Talon, Elizabeth is very tight here. I would suggest you start using anal plugs to stretch her bottom," Doc suggested as he moved his finger in and out of her.

The heat already building in her body because of the exam burst into flames. The exploring touch and the knowledge her Daddy would pay attention to her bottom combined to make her juices flow liberally. *Please don't let the paper get wet. Maybe they won't notice?*

"Press the thermometer into her bottom until you reach resistance. Then, hold it there for several seconds. When you see or feel her relax, adjust the placement. The device will measure most accurately when inserted deeply," Doc instructed. "Leave it in place for ten minutes or longer."

Elizabeth squeezed her eyelids shut as Doc twirled the intruder inside her. Each time, it seemed to move a bit further inside. She tried to distract herself so she wouldn't think about how erotic it was to have something in her bottom. The image of Talon lubricating a large plug to go in her bottom popped into her brain. What made it even sexier was she knew he would follow through on Doc's advice. He would pay attention to her bottom regularly. She pulled Borscht close as she moaned softly in arousal.

"Little girls have very sensitive bottoms. Your Little is very responsive. You are a very lucky man," Doc complimented.

Talon smoothed a hand over her hip. "I know."

Finally, Doc removed the device from her bottom and announced the results. "Perfect. I will give her some medicine because she's congested, though."

A smaller tip poked into her opening and Elizabeth felt a stream of liquid flow inside. She immediately clenched her buttocks, but it was too late. The medicine was inside.

"Let that sit inside her for as long as possible. Perhaps a nap after the exam would be best," Doc suggested as he peeled off his gloves to throw them in the trash. "Alright, Little one. Roll on your back. I need to check a couple more areas before we're done."

Cautiously, Elizabeth followed his directions. Talon helped her by adjusting the towel to stretch over her front.

Doc opened a cabinet and withdrew a wedge-shaped pillow. "We'll prop up her bottom a bit to help the medicine flow deep. Would you lift Elizabeth's hips for me?" the medic requested.

Talon squeezed her hand before sliding his hands under her bottom. He lifted her lower half above the table while Doc placed the pillow under the paper protecting the exam table.

"That's perfect. Talon, you need to examine Elizabeth's breasts every month. It's best right after her period so her breasts will be less tender. Stand behind your Little's head for this next part so you can see best."

"Elizabeth, you are doing such a great job. I'm very proud of you. Reach your hands up to your Daddy," Doc requested.

When she followed his instructions, Talon set Borscht by her face before linking his hands with hers and pressing them to the top of the table above her head. Elizabeth squirmed when Doc folded the towel down to below her waist.

"Nooooo," she wailed.

"I know. This is hard for Little girls. You'll be okay. Your

Daddy is holding your hands. He's not going to let anything happen to you. He needs to know how to protect you."

"First, look at Elizabeth's breasts, checking for dimples, swelling, or visible lumps. If there are any changes, let me know."

Elizabeth struggled to hold still as both men focused on her breasts. When Doc moved several seconds later to examine her, she almost breathed a sigh of relief until he touched her.

Doc pressed his fingers against one breast and moved in a clockwise fashion around the mound, looking for anything concerning as he described in detail what he was doing for Talon's reference. Elizabeth had a difficult time listening to his directions. She could only focus on his probing touch. He finished by squeezing and pulling on her nipple before checking the other side.

"Everything feels great, Elizabeth. Almost done," Doc promised as he removed the towel from her body, leaving her naked on the table.

"Wait!"

"Just a few minutes, Elizabeth. Would having your stuffie back make you feel better?" Doc asked.

"Y... Yes," she said, knowing her voice revealed her emotions.

"Then, let's make that happen."

Doc looked up at Talon. "You can release her hands. She's going to be a good girl, I can tell."

Elizabeth nodded without really knowing what she was promising to behave for, and her Daddy released her hands.

Free, Elizabeth pulled Borscht to her chest to cuddle. Suspicious, she watched as Doc motioned Talon to the side of the table.

"We'll shift her body to the bottom edge of the table," Doc instructed.

The two men slid their hands under the cushion and her upper back and moved her down the exam table. Talon followed

Doc's movements as the medic bent her legs and secured them into the stirrups he pulled from below the surface of the table. Elizabeth tried to kick her legs free but the straps around her ankles and upper calves held her firmly in place.

"You don't have to tie me," Elizabeth complained.

Both men just looked at her to remind her they'd just seen her try to get loose. "You'll be safe now, Little one," Doc said in an even tone.

He stepped between her widely stretched legs and motioned Talon to move closer. With a click, Doc turned on a standing lamp. Adjusting it so the light fell on her most private area, Elizabeth knew they could both see how wet she was as well as everything else about her.

I'm never going to be able to look at Doc again.

"You had sex last night?" Doc asked as he pulled on gloves.

Elizabeth wanted the earth to open and swallow her up. Talon answered him easily.

"Three times last night. She did soak in a warm bath this morning."

"Smart. Another bath tonight wouldn't hurt. Her tissues are still enflamed," Doc said, stroking her inner labia with his fingers as he probed for tender spots. "She lubricates well, but you may wish to add more during prolonged love making."

"Gotcha," Talon said and noted it on his phone as Doc sat down between her thighs.

"You'll feel my fingers enter your vagina, Elizabeth. Try to relax."

After a careful digital exam, Doc stood and ran the warm water before holding a plastic device Elizabeth hated in the flow. Retaking his seat, he warned, "Now, I'll insert the speculum."

Elizabeth sighed with relief. It wasn't the cold metal thing her regular doctor used. The warmed one was invasive but not shiver inducing.

"Your cervix looks good. Are you up to date on your pap smears?" he asked.

"I just had it a couple months ago," she assured him.

"Good girl," Doc praised her as he withdrew the speculum. "I'm all done. That didn't hurt, did it?"

"No," she whispered, and Doc rewarded her with a pat on her inner thigh.

"Let me get you cleaned up, and you'll be ready to head back to your apartment for a nap," Doc suggested.

Before she could protest that she could take care of herself, Doc grabbed a moistened wipe. He had all the lubricant and juices from between her thighs, buttocks, and even the tops of her thighs cleaned quickly.

Soon, the men released her legs and Talon scooped her up in his arms. Doc draped the towel over her body so she wouldn't get cold in the hall and opened the door. Her Daddy carried Elizabeth and Borscht back to their apartment and straight to bed.

"Naptime, Little girl. How about I read you a story?"

"I'm not tired, Daddy," she protested.

"We'll see," he suggested, pulling a book from the shelf under the nightstand.

Elizabeth didn't see any of the pictures after the first three pages.

CHAPTER
EIGHTEEN

That evening at dinner, Elizabeth was starving. She ate three of Gabriel's famous tacos and a pile of the best guacamole she'd ever eaten.

Harper leaned over to whisper in her ear, "Daddy's bottom treatment makes me hungry, too."

Elizabeth's jaw dropped open. After she got over her shock, Elizabeth whispered back, "How does he know?"

"Just be glad he's not your Daddy," Harper said with a smile, showing Elizabeth she didn't mind Doc's treatments at all.

"I feel so much better," Elizabeth confessed.

"Me, too. We all do," Harper shared.

"You're not mad he examined me?" Elizabeth felt she had to check.

"Not at all. Because I know he made you better."

Impulsively, Elizabeth leaned over to hug Harper. "What a special person," she thought before realizing Harper didn't have anything to worry about. Just as Doc had said, her Daddy loved her above all things.

Arms wrapped around Harper from the other side. Elizabeth looked up to see Ivy grinning at her as she joined the hug. Elizabeth couldn't help but smile back.

"You're hugging me to death," Harper called, laughing. She squeaked when Ivy and Elizabeth squeezed her tighter before releasing her.

"What are you hugging Harper for?" Elizabeth leaned forward to ask Ivy.

"She's my friend. Everyone can always use a hug," Ivy explained.

Elizabeth nodded in agreement. That made perfect sense. Hugs were important. She liked that the Littles all enjoyed each other's company. They all had different interests and personalities but were incredibly similar in the most important ways.

Leaning the other way, she propped herself against Talon's shoulder. Without interrupting his conversation with Storm, her Daddy slid his chair back and scooped her onto his lap. When she was settled, Talon scooped a chip into his guacamole and lifted it to her lips. Without hesitating, Elizabeth opened her mouth to devour the treat as she eavesdropped on her Daddy's conversation.

"Those fucking rims we got in are all jacked up," Storm shared. "We'll have to send them back."

"Storm, you owe ten dollars to the swear jar," Remi told him before jumping up to bring it to him. "I don't want you to forget."

"Of course, you don't," Storm groused before digging his money out of his pocket. He tucked a twenty into the jar and told her, "I'll pay in advance."

"Good idea. Thank you, Storm," Remi said politely, before turning and giggling all the way back to put the jar away.

Talon laughed and fed another bite to Elizabeth as the conversation changed to something that had happened at the shop. Elizabeth tuned out automatically. She knew nothing about motorcycles or repairs.

As she chewed, Elizabeth looked around the large gathering room. There were people playing pool, eating, and hanging around the bar chatting. The conversations made it a noisy but comfortable rumble. She was amazed how comfortable she felt sitting on Talon's lap. No one gave them a second look.

"More?"

Elizabeth looked back at Talon to see another guacamole offering. "No, thank you. I'm stuffed."

"I'm glad you were hungry," he answered and winked.

She knew immediately he was celebrating how well her doctor's visit had gone. Before she could be embarrassed, Elizabeth felt a tap on her shoulder. Turning, she saw Eden behind her.

"We're going into the library. Want to come?" Eden invited.

"Oh, yes!"

After twisting around to give her Daddy a kiss on the cheek, she scrambled off his lap. Immediately, the Littles surrounded her as they moved to their own gathering place. Everyone dropped to the floor in a big circle.

"Who do we want to invite to read us a story?" Remi asked.

"Bear," Carlee suggested. "He's never read us a story. I can tell he'd be a good story reader. Let's choose a book with a bear in it so he can be all growly."

"That's an amazing idea!" Ivy cheered.

Harper and Elizabeth were the closest to the bookshelf. They rose to their knees to look at their choices. After conferring together, they turned around to show the group their suggestion. It was a story about a bear dad who lost his cub in the woods and set off to find him.

"That's a perfect story!" Eden cheered.

"Who's going to go ask him? Anyone want to volunteer?" Remi looked around the group.

Elizabeth held up her hand. "I'll go if no one else wants to."

"Perfect. Do you know who Bear is?" Harper double checked. "There's a lot of names to remember."

"He's the big guy with dark hair," Ivy said, pointing to a burly guy talking to Gabriel.

Used to holding her own against the toughest lawyers in

town, Elizabeth felt a bit nervous as she stood up while holding the book to her chest. That nervous feeling grew as she got closer to the two men.

"Um, hi!" she said to interrupt them.

"Hi, Elizabeth. Are you having fun with the other Littles?" Gabriel asked with a smile.

"Yes. They're all really nice."

Bear said, "I'm glad."

"They sent me over here to ask if you'd read a book for us," Elizabeth confessed.

"I'd love to read a book," Gabriel volunteered.

"Oh! I'm sorry. I was supposed to ask Bear." Elizabeth rushed to correct the misunderstanding.

"It's a story about a growly bear," she explained, holding up the book so they could see the cover.

"That's totally you," Gabriel said, thumping Bear on the back. "I agree, Elizabeth. Bear is the perfect Shadowridge Guardian to read *that* book."

She nodded, happy that Gabriel understood. "I'll have them find a book for you to read next time," she promised.

"I'll look forward to it. Have fun, Bear."

As they got closer to the library, Elizabeth looked at the room and Bear's bulk. Would he fit inside? Where was he going to sit?

When they arrived, everyone scooted around to leave a big space for Bear to sit on a large cushion. To Elizabeth's surprise, he folded his large frame easily to the floor and held out a hand for the book as he greeted everyone.

"Hi! Thank you for asking me to come read to you. I hear you chose a special book for me to read."

Everyone looked at Elizabeth and she realized she still had the book. "Oops. Sorry." She passed the book to Bear.

"No sorries needed," he assured her.

Bear looked at the cover and the title. "This book looks amazing. Let's get started."

Opening the cover, he read, "'Barley? Where are you, little cub?' roared her father."

Bear pointed out the worried look on the big bear's face. He had the Littles scan the picture to see if they could tell where Barley had gone.

"That bush looks funny," Eden pointed out. "It's divided in the middle like something walked through it."

"Good eyes, Eden. Let's find out if Barley went that way," Bear suggested, turning the page.

The Littles leaned forward eagerly to see what would happen next. Elizabeth couldn't wait to see the next picture.

"Look, there's a bunch of bees flying around!" she said in excitement.

"Oh, no! Barley tried to raid the bee's nest. They didn't like that," Bear read for them.

"I know where Barley goes next!" Remi joined in the fun. "There's a path of trampled dandelions going that way!"

"But there's ripples in the pond. Which way did Barley go?" Ivy asked.

Slowly, Bear led them through the dad bear's trek to find his lost cub. On each page, they looked at all the clues and followed the path. Elizabeth was aware of several of the Littles' Daddies stopping by to check on everyone and then standing quietly to listen to the story.

When Bear turned the last page to show Barley in her daddy's arms, the Littles all cheered, "Hooray!"

"Look! She has twigs in her fur!" Carlee said.

"And scales on one paw," Eden shared. "She did eat that fish."

As they all pointed out different things they saw, Elizabeth heard Talon whisper to Gabriel, "Did you see that coming?"

"The dad bear finding his cub? Of course," Gabriel answered in surprise.

"No. Bear skunking all of us at story reading," Talon joked.

"He's going to have to give us lessons," Steele suggested.

"For God's sake, never tell the Devil's Jesters we're taking story-telling lessons," Gabriel suggested.

"You've got my oath," Talon promised. Then he said a bit louder, "Watch this. How many Littles will it take to heave Bear off that cushion?"

"Smart ass," Bear responded. "Come give me a hand."

Gabriel and Talon walked forward to offer Bear their hands. Together, they yanked the muscular man to his feet.

"Thanks," Bear said gruffly.

"Hey. That was a good job reading," Gabriel complimented him.

"It was awesome," Eden enthused, throwing her arms around Gabriel's waist to hug him.

"I'm glad you liked it, ladybug," Gabriel replied, rubbing her back as he hugged her.

"I loved it, too," Elizabeth said as she joined them, taking her Daddy's hand and squeezing it.

Motioning Talon to lean closer, she whispered, "You don't need to take lessons."

He rewarded her with a kiss that made her toes curl upward in happiness.

CHAPTER
NINETEEN

Monday was a day from hell. Everything that could go wrong did—including a power outage at the courthouse that canceled everything for the afternoon. Returning to her office, Elizabeth tried to get everything rescheduled in her already packed schedule and groaned at the look of her now back-to-back appointments that would make her life even more challenging.

I'll have to eat flavored gelatin or a smoothie for lunch. There won't be any time to chew.

Shaking her head, she didn't even want to think about how much her feet would hurt as she raced around trying to appear in all the courtrooms. When she'd finished everything she could do, Elizabeth grabbed her phone to text the Littles. Maybe someone could join her for a late lunch.

Eden immediately answered. "I'm starving. Can we go to The Hangout for nachos? I haven't had them in forever."

"That sounds amazing! See you there in twenty minutes?" Elizabeth suggested.

"Perfect."

With the conversation in the chat, Elizabeth knew the others could read and join them if they were free. She walked to her car, scanning the area. Elizabeth hadn't recovered yet from the Devil's Jesters treatment of her. Even now that she knew why they'd harassed her, she didn't let her guard down.

Passing several people headed toward the courtroom, she didn't warn them. They'd want to check in at the desk to register their effort to be there for their cases. She reached her car and jumped in.

Traffic was light and Elizabeth arrived at The Hangout early. She thought about calling her Daddy but didn't want him to tell her to come home early. Maybe she'd text him later and ask him to come dance.

Walking into the restaurant, she greeted the hostess. "Hi. Could I have a table for four? There's only two of us coming but more may join us."

"Fun! It sounds like a party brewing. How about if I put you at this table for four that has a two-person table on each side. Then you can expand it as needed."

"That's amazing. Thank you." Elizabeth expressed her appreciation with a smile.

"Of course."

A few minutes later, the cute redhead Elizabeth was expecting walked in with a long-haired brunette. Elizabeth waved. "Eden! Harper! Over here."

"Hi, Elizabeth," Harper greeted her when they got to the table and gave her a hug before sliding into a seat as Eden hugged Elizabeth as well.

"Hey! This is a great table. It's not on the dance floor so the music is not as loud, but we can see the whole place," Eden said as she looked around.

"And we can expand, if anyone else decides to join us."

"I think everyone else is working but who knows? How in the world did you get the afternoon off?" Harper asked.

"Power outage at the courthouse," she answered.

"Hooray! Let's eat, drink, and be merry!"

One margarita each and a ton of nachos later, the three sat back and looked at the almost empty platter.

"I can't believe we ate all that," Eden groaned.

"It's a good thing the others couldn't join us. They would have had to order their own nachos," Harper joked.

"Can I get you anything else, ladies?" the server asked.

"No, thank you. Just the bill," Elizabeth requested. "Talon will wonder where I am."

Looking around at the people just beginning to gather, Elizabeth's eyes were drawn to a distinctive, tattooed figure on the dance floor. Elizabeth recognized him immediately. She raised her arm to wave to him and froze as a slender brunette ran to jump into his arms. The flash of Talon's pearly whites clued her in that he was happy to see the woman in his arms. She dropped her arm and tried to come up with an explanation.

"Your face just went white. What's wrong?" Eden asked.

She thought about lying but couldn't. "Look out on the dance floor." Elizabeth nodded in that direction.

The couple danced now, Talon leading his partner with skill and the smoothness of a professionally trained dancer. The woman in his arms was incredible. Light and flexible, she was a dancer's dream partner. Talon led her easily through a maze of complex moves and turns.

"Is that Talon?" Harper asked. "Who's that with him?"

"I don't know," Elizabeth answered as she watched him kiss the woman's forehead just as he did hers when she pleased him.

"Um. I have to get out of here before he sees me. I wasn't here, okay?" she said, fishing in her purse for her wallet. She pulled out three twenties and placed them on the table.

"That should cover my share. Thank you for meeting me here. I've enjoyed knowing you," Elizabeth said as she stood.

"That sounds like you won't talk to us anymore. We'll see you back at the compound," Harper corrected her.

"I won't be there. Bye," she said quickly before she burst into tears. Turning, she walked out of the building and flew across the parking lot to her car.

Tears threatened to blur her eyes as she drove home to her apartment. Menaced by heavy traffic, Elizabeth kept a solid grip on her emotions as she negotiated the packed highway. Finally, she reached her exit and broke away from the mass movement of cars to a relatively calm street.

A single tear ran down her cheek followed by another and another. Pulling into her assigned parking spot, Elizabeth covered her face with her hands. How had she found two unfaithful men?

At least he had his clothes on this time.

That thought just made her cry harder. Her phone rang in her purse, and Elizabeth didn't even look to see who was on the line. She couldn't.

About ten minutes later, she forced herself to open her car door and head up to her apartment. Opening the door, she looked around at the abandoned space. It almost looked like one of those places staged for a quick sale, except hers had a few personal possessions here and there.

Personal possessions. The words echoed in her brain and she started crying again. She had to rescue Puff and Borscht. They were at Talon's apartment in the Shadowridge Guardians complex.

Thank goodness they weren't at his house in the country. She'd never get in there. If she went to his apartment in the compound now, Talon would still be dancing with that woman. Elizabeth could grab her stuff and leave. "I'll have to come up with an excuse," she thought as she grabbed her keys and darted back out the door.

"Hey, Storm. Just darting in to pick up something I promised to show to Ivy."

"Ivy? She's still at the bank," Storm told her.

"I know. That's why I'm here now," she told him as she hurried into the hallway.

Congratulating herself on the lie she'd concocted, Elizabeth hurried into Talon's apartment. She held onto the bed as she dropped to her knees to grab her suitcase from under the bed.

The door opening made her panic. Elizabeth flattened herself on the floor and scooted under the bed to hide. It was tight, but she fit. *Oh my god. What if he brought her back here?* Her stomach churned as she looked up at the bed above her.

"Elizabeth? Buttercup? Are you in here?"

Two sets of footsteps sounded on the floor. He wasn't alone.

Holding her breath, she watched his boots wander through the apartment even checking in the closet and the shower. *Please think I went out the back door. Please think I'm driving away now.*

"Are you sure that was her car?" a feminine voice asked.

"Definitely. Her briefcase was inside. I'll call her."

After a second of sheer panic, Elizabeth realized she'd forgotten her phone in her car. It wouldn't give her away. She blew out her breath silently in relief. Hearing the door open, she sagged against the floor. That feeling didn't last for long.

"Storm? Are you sure you talked to my Elizabeth?" Talon called from the doorway into the hallway.

"Petite, blonde, dressed in a power suit. She's been the one sitting on your lap and giving you hugs, right?" Storm joked. "Is she playing hide and seek?"

"I don't know. Did she look upset?" he asked.

"Stressed. She had that line between her eyes," Storm said, and Elizabeth imagined him drawing a vertical line between his eyebrows. That was her worst stress wrinkle.

"That sounds like Elizabeth. She wasn't in the library, was she?"

"Nope. It's quiet in there today. I just got a bottle of water from the fridge, and it was empty," Storm reported.

"Could you help me knock on doors and see if she's visiting someone?"

"Of course."

Elizabeth stayed where she was until she heard the guys in the hallway going from door to door, searching for her.

Slowly, she slid out from under the bed and grabbed Puff and Borscht from the cozy spot she'd left them. Everything else didn't matter. She just needed her stuffies. Pausing to listen, she noticed their voices were much quieter. The guys must have turned the corner. This was her chance. She darted to the door.

"Hi. You aren't leaving now, are you?"

Elizabeth whirled at the sound of the woman's voice. Sitting with her legs tucked underneath her in the corner of couch sat a woman with brown hair and almost black eyes. "Yes. I'm leaving now."

"I think Talon wanted to introduce us."

The woman gracefully uncurled herself from the couch to approach Elizabeth and hold out her hand. "I'm Margaret."

"I can't touch your hand. I'll throw up. How can you be so brazen?"

Elizabeth reached for the doorknob behind her and opened the door. She dashed out, only to smash into a hard obstacle. The two stuffies tumbled to the ground as the air rushed out of her lungs. Looking up, Elizabeth saw Ivy's Daddy. Dragging oxygen into her lungs, she scrambled to pick up Puff and Borscht. Elizabeth forced words out of her mouth. "Dammit, Steele. Don't block the hallway."

"Grab her," Talon called, and Steele's hands closed around Elizabeth's shoulders, holding her in place.

"Steele, he's cheating on me. Let me go!" Elizabeth pleaded.

"Talon? You're cheating on her?" the woman now standing in the doorway asked.

"No, I'm not cheating on her. The only other woman I've

hung out with since I met Elizabeth is you," Talon explained as he jogged down the hallway to reach Elizabeth.

He stroked a hand down her back, and she couldn't help flinching away.

"Let. Me. Go."

The absolute power in her voice made Steele lift his hands from her body and step back. "Sorry, Elizabeth. Listen to him, please."

"I listened to one man explain how it was my fault he cheated on me. I'm not listening to another. Go back to that floozy you spent your afternoon with," she said, mentally pulling the shreds of her dignity around herself as she shifted to the side to step around Steele.

"That was my mother, Elizabeth," Talon said quietly from behind her.

Elizabeth turned her head to stare at the woman who looked at her with such concern. "Your mother?" she repeated. "I saw you dancing together. You moved so well together. Like you'd known each other for years."

"Twenty-five years," the woman filled in for her. "I'm so sorry we scared you. Would you stay so we can get acquainted? I've been looking forward to meeting the woman who captured my son's heart."

"I feel so stupid. It's probably best that I leave," Elizabeth said, shaking her head.

"It's all my fault," Margaret said quickly. "I showed up without any notice to see if I could sweet talk my son into dancing with me at a ballroom competition. His father sprained his ankle and will be on crutches for a week."

"I thought of the big dance floor at The Hangout. We went to practice there this afternoon and came back here so Mom could meet you when you got off work. I texted you."

"I haven't looked at my phone."

"I'm sorry, Buttercup. I don't want you to be hurt even by a misunderstanding. Can I hug you now?" he asked, stepping closer.

"I think I'd like that," she answered, walking forward into his arms.

"Margaret, can I offer you a drink or some water?" Steele asked diplomatically.

"I think a drink is a great idea," Margaret answered.

Soon, they were alone in the hallway.

"Your mother thinks I'm an idiot," Elizabeth whispered.

"She absolutely does not. I'm good at reading my mom. She was tickled you loved me so much you wouldn't settle for something less than all my love," Talon assured her.

"She doesn't look old enough to be your mother."

"You should tell her that. She's already going to kick my butt for worrying you. You might as well make her your best friend with that compliment. She'll make me dance the Paso Doble for punishment and I hate the Paso Doble."

Elizabeth looked up to meet his gaze. His dark eyes twinkled with love and relief. "I'm sorry I panicked."

"It must have looked bad. I'm sorry. I am excited for you to meet my mother and my father someday when he is mobile," Talon said. "Running and not talking to me was the worst way to handle this. I want you to promise me you'll talk to me if you ever get upset."

When she hesitated, he added, "I'm not your absolute bastard of an ex-husband."

Elizabeth shook her head. "I know it isn't fair to judge your actions by the history of his. He hurt me so bad, and it came out of the blue. I didn't have any inkling that he was cheating. So when I saw you dancing, I thought it was happening again."

"It's never going to happen, Little girl. I love you. No one else."

"You're only twenty-five. You may change your mind." Elizabeth reached up to trace that line Storm had noticed. "When my wrinkle has a lot more friends."

"You're a few years older than I am. Not decades. I have some wrinkles, too. You are gorgeous today and you'll be gorgeous when you're seventy. I'm never going to change my mind. You are my Little girl."

She nodded and pressed her cheek to his chest, hearing his heart beat. "I love being your Little girl."

"When you're ready, we'll get married."

"Married?" she repeated, looking up at him.

"I'm never going to let you go, Buttercup. Now I know to check under beds," he said, brushing the dust from her suit. "I would have searched from one side of this city to the next and further if I'd needed to. You are mine."

"And you're mine," she pointed out.

"Definitely."

"Would you introduce me to your mother so I can apologize?" Elizabeth asked.

"I will. You don't need to apologize..."

Talon stopped to listen to the music that had just begun in the common room. "Oh, crap. She's playing a Paso Doble already."

"I can't wait to see this," Elizabeth said, starting down the hall.

"Save me now," Talon moaned as he followed her.

CHAPTER
TWENTY

The exhibition hall was packed with people buzzing with excitement. As Steele led the way through those gathered, a path formed for the Shadowridge Guardians decked out in their cuts and worn jeans. The doorman had attempted to school Steele on the dress requirement to attend a dance competition but quickly made an exception when he looked past the MC's president to see a line of huge men waiting to get in. The women accompanying them were perfectly attired and so excited.

"Hold onto my hand," Ink said firmly to Elizabeth. "If I lose you, Talon will kick my butt."

"I was just going to talk to Remi. I love her black dress," Elizabeth explained.

"We'll go over there together," Ink decreed and steered her toward her friend.

"I'm not going to run away," Elizabeth assured him.

"If Talon finds us and you're not with me, it won't just be my butt getting Talon's wrath," Ink reminded her.

"Oh. Good point. I'll stay with you," she promised.

"What are those pants Talon is wearing?" Faust asked, using his height advantage to look over the crowd.

"Is he out there warming up?" Elizabeth asked, rising to her tiptoes to try and see.

"Here, Little girl," Ink said as he pulled her close to lift her up.

"I see him! Those pants look hot on him, Faust. Not everyone could rock them like that," Elizabeth defended her Daddy.

"I want to see," Harper demanded, and Doc lifted her to see as well. "Oh, yeah. He looks good in those."

"Stop ogling Talon in his fancy dance pants," Doc said sternly.

"Look, everyone is sitting down," Elizabeth pointed out.

"I'll be damned." Steele cursed in front of her, drawing the horrified attention of the people who'd dared sit next to the bikers.

Elizabeth followed his line of vision to see another set of leather-clad guys entering. The Devil's Jesters had arrived. She waved to capture their attention and pointed to empty seats around them.

"What did you do?" Steele asked, his low voice filled with concern.

"Slash's daughter takes ballroom classes. She'd never been to a performance, so I invited them. They promised to be on their best behavior. And Slash is still under scrutiny for having custody of his kids. Don't worry. They'll behave."

Ink's large frame shook with laughter. "We've both officially damaged our bad-ass reputations." The humor spread through the gathered Shadowridge Guardians and Littles.

The lights darkened and spotlights twirled around the dance floor, making everyone hush. When the first dancers stepped onto the floor, Elizabeth clutched the program as she watched. Her Daddy and his mother would dance third in this round.

"I think I'm in love," Ink whispered, focused on the form-revealing costume of the first female dancer.

"Shh!" Elizabeth hissed and then almost giggled as Ink drew his fingers over his lips, officially zipping them shut.

A motion caught her eye and she turned to see Faust lift a pair of fancy opera glasses to his eyes. Where in the world had he gotten those? Elizabeth shook her head. She couldn't wait to see what happened when those two met their Littles. Crossing her fingers, she sent out a wish into the world that each of the Shadowridge Guardians would find their perfect match.

"And next on the floor is our beloved Margaret Deveraux. Her usual partner could not be with us tonight due to injury. It is a true pleasure to have her son, Theodore Deveraux, a three-time world champion, dancing with her tonight," the announcer broadcast.

Theodore. Elizabeth grinned. She had her own real-life teddy.

"That's Talon's mother?" Kade asked, drawing her attention back to the dance floor.

Elizabeth saw Remi elbow him and mentally applauded her friend before focusing back on the couple. Margaret looked amazing. Her fit dancer's body still turned heads as she strutted on those impossibly high heels across the floor. Elizabeth understood why she'd mistaken her for a rival.

Elizabeth moved to the edge of her chair as Talon and Margaret took their places in front of the judges. The music swelled and she couldn't help but smile. The Paso Doble. She clapped her hand over her mouth as Talon became the matador, his movements strong and forceful.

She glared at the woman in front of her who dared to sigh in delight. Talon was *her* Daddy.

Ink's hand wrapped around her knee, holding her in place. Elizabeth forced herself to relax. She had to admit that Talon affected her the same way. And Elizabeth got to take him home.

At the intermission, two children rushed down the row of Shadowridge bikers to throw their arms around Elizabeth's waist.

"Hello, Jalinda and Jerome. I'm so glad to see you here," Elizabeth greeted Slash's children, whom she'd met several times at the office.

"Thank you so much for the tickets. I'm having the best time," Jalinda told her.

"Me, too," echoed Jerome.

"I love this. Who do you think will win?" Elizabeth asked.

"Talon, of course. He's the best," Jerome said without hesitating.

"I think so, too. Let's keep our fingers crossed," she suggested, holding up her hands to show her gestures.

"We'll do it. Daddy's waiting for us," Jalinda said before they turned to rush back to their father.

Slash's demeanor toward Elizabeth had definitely changed after she had connected him with a good lawyer in her firm. Nothing could ever erase the terror the Devil's Jesters had put her through or make the two MCs completely trust each other, but for now there was a truce. She nodded when Slash mouthed his thanks.

"Look, Elizabeth," Ivy urged, pointing at a man approaching. Many people in the crowd patted him on the back and shook his hand. There were even a few hussies who took selfies with him.

"D... Talon!" Elizabeth called and rushed to meet him.

"Hi, Little girl."

Talon wrapped an arm around her and hugged her close. He looked over the mass of Guardians who had shown up to support him and said, "Thank you all for coming. I'm never going to hear the end of this, am I?"

"Never," Faust assured him.

"I can live with that," Talon said with a grin that made Elizabeth's heart beat faster.

"Are you having fun? You're doing so well," Elizabeth asked.

"My blisters have blisters, but we're dancing well together," Talon assured her.

"Maybe I should take some of those dance lessons," Rock suggested, running his hand thoughtfully over his graying beard.

"Just have the ladies wear steel-toed boots," Atlas suggested.

"We could take lessons, Daddy," Carlee suggested.

"I'll buy you some boots, Carlee. I'd hate for someone I cherish to lose a toe," Rock teased.

"Rock!" Carlee said, rolling her eyes.

"I have to get back. I just wanted to check on the leather-wearing hooligans who'd invaded the ballroom dance event. The organizers panicked until Margaret assured them you'd behave," Talon shared with a laugh.

He turned to say privately to Elizabeth, "Stay with Ink. It will take a while for me to get to you after the winners are announced."

"I will. Promise." She raised her still crossed fingers to make an X over her chest.

"Good girl."

Elizabeth watched the crowd clump together and knew Talon was on his way to her. He and Margaret had won the competition easily. When they finally appeared, Margaret wore a simple wrap-around dress that looked elegant on her. Talon had transformed himself from the dramatic makeup and costumes he'd worn to his boots, jeans, and cut.

"Congratulations!" Elizabeth called, rushing to his side. "You both danced amazingly."

"Thank you, Elizabeth. I appreciate you letting me borrow Talon for the competition," Margaret said with a smile.

"Hi, Buttercup." Talon greeted her with a kiss. He looked tired but happy.

Keeping Elizabeth at his side, Talon handed over a stack of business cards and promotional postcards to Steele. "All these people are interested in joining the Shadowridge Guardians," he shared.

"Do they expect we'll have a dance team now?" Steele growled as he looked through the cards.

"Probably. Don't worry. All the dancers will forget about us by next week. I told everyone the first step was to check the requirements online and fill out the application. That will weed out some more," Talon predicted.

"I'm starving. I don't suppose anyone knows how to grill at that clubhouse of yours," Margaret asked.

"Definitely," Gabriel assured her. "Let's head back there for a celebration."

"Only if you promise not to play Paso Doble music," Talon warned.

"I won't ask them to play anything," Margaret assured him. "Can I catch a ride with one of you? I took a ride share from my hotel."

Ink stepped forward to extend his arm. With her hand wrapped around his bicep, he led the way to where their bikes were parked.

"He remembers she's married, right?" Talon asked, watching them walk away.

"He does. Don't worry about your mom. Ink will take good care of her," Elizabeth assured him. "Or we could swap and I could hold onto Ink on the way home."

"Mom will be fine. You're riding with me." Talon nixed that idea.

"I should learn to dance like your mom so we could dance together," Elizabeth blurted. She'd been worried Talon would want someone talented to compete with.

"You can take lessons if that is what you wish. I think we dance perfectly together already, Little girl. I'm not interested in competing anymore. Today was fun to help my mom but it takes more time than I'm willing to commit."

"I probably couldn't dance as well as your mother."

"Hey. My mom started dance lessons at two. She entered her first competition when she was five. I'll let her tell you how old she is, but she's danced all my life, so you know that's over twenty-five years. I would never expect or want you to train for competition dancing."

"You mean, I'm too old."

"Not to dance with me and have fun at The Hangout. That's all I'm interested in—enjoying my gorgeous Little. Besides, I'd never let you past our door with those skimpy outfits on," Talon told her.

"I'd have to keep everything shaved," she teased.

"And I'd have to kill all the men in the audience. Steele frowns on violence inside the MC."

"We better avoid that then. You'll teach me more of your fun dance moves?" she asked.

"I can't wait."

CHAPTER
TWENTY-ONE

E lizabeth walked halfway across the parking lot before stopping. There were seven members of the Devil's Jesters arranged around her car. Instantly, her heart rate sped up.

"I thought we were past this," she called as she selected Talon's number on her phone. Without hesitating, she called it and touched the speaker button when he answered. "Talon, the Devil's Jesters are here."

Elizabeth ignored the slew of questions that followed, only answering two. "I'm safe and in the south parking lot."

"The verdict came in this afternoon. My in-laws will receive supervised visits when they arrange them two weeks in advance. Jalinda and Jerome will remain living with me," Slash reported in a booming voice.

"I'm glad the kids get to stay with you," she said with a smile.

"Me, too. Tell that man of yours our truce is over. The Guardians need to keep their eyes peeled for the Devil's Jesters," Slash told her before taking a swig from a bottle she recognized as whiskey.

"You know the social workers will be checking in on you for

months, right? Me telling them you're driving under the influence will not be viewed positively." Elizabeth hardened her voice to the one she used in court. "Any threat to me would also trigger a review by the judge."

"That doesn't stop me," Vengeance yelled, taking a step forward.

"It does, Marion," she said evenly.

"Marion?" One of the Jesters laughed at the name. "Who's Marion?"

"That's Vengeance's birth name, Lester," Elizabeth informed the sneering man, providing his name as well. "Yes, that's right. I have everyone's information on file in my office with a note to my assistant to turn that over to the police and search for you all first if anything happens to me."

"They won't believe you. We have friends in the force," Vengeance blustered.

Hearing the rumble of approaching motorcycles, she maintained her bravado. "Picture this, guys. We're standing in court and my lawyer asks me to stand up next to you. Five foot three inches vs six foot eight inches. And behind the bench? A female judge who went to law school with me. Whose friends are going to be the most help?"

They tried to look nonchalant but there was a light dawning in their eyes. The Devil's Jesters might be unlawful thugs, but they knew when pursuing something would result in a serious loss of freedom. They exchanged glances for the first time.

Elizabeth didn't relax her guard. She'd never be able to do that. Mentally shrugging, she'd given up the right to walk through life without looking over her shoulder every few steps. Her job provided challenges and earned her enemies. She could live with that, knowing she helped people who otherwise wouldn't have any hope.

Four sleek, well-ridden motorcycles roared into the parking lot. Talon, Bear, Faust, and Storm kicked down their stands and dismounted. Talon claimed the spot next to Elizabeth with the others backing up the duo.

"This is getting old, Slash," Talon told him with a tone of absolute boredom.

"We're so sorry to inconvenience you," Slash told him with a sneer.

"I'm going to say this slowly so you'll understand. A move against any of our women will bring unlimited wrath onto your MC. This ends today. Now."

"We're shaking in our boots," Slash mocked. He did look over his shoulder to nod at the bikers backing him up. One by one, they mounted their bikes and took off. Their bravado never wavered, but it was obvious they'd backed down.

When the parking lot was empty, Talon looked over his shoulders at the Guardians who had jumped at the opportunity to ride with him. He shrugged his shoulders and turned to Elizabeth.

"You'd already scared the crap out of them, hadn't you?"

"I just pointed out a few things and let them connect the dots," she shared.

"I'm glad your Little's on our side," Faust stated with an almost smile tilting up the corners of his mouth.

"Awww. I like you, too, Faust." Elizabeth smiled fondly back at him.

Shaking his head, the perpetual mean guy walked back to his bike and got back on.

"Let's go, Buttercup. We'll escort you home," Talon told her.

"Like my own motorcade. Neat!" She ran for her car and jumped inside.

"We're going to have to repeat this for each Little now," Bear pointed out.

"I know. There's only six. That's not too much effort. Maybe we can double up a few," Talon suggested as they walked back to join Faust.

"There's only six, *now*," Storm pointed out.

"What? You can sense more coming in the wind?" Bear joked.

"Yes. They're out there. We just have to find them."

After dinner that night, Elizabeth jotted down the incident and the date in the Little's secret journal in the library amongst lots of laughter after telling them all what really happened. "I think they'll back off but who knows with those guys. Watch your backs," she warned as she met each Little's gaze.

It was unbelievable to know just how much she enjoyed and cared for each of these women. They were all so different but so similar.

"Thanks for welcoming me," Elizabeth said simply.

"You're one of us," Ivy told her without hesitation. "I'm trying to figure out who will be the next one to meet their Little."

"Think Rock would ever be interested in someone again?" Carlee asked, turning to Remi.

"I don't know. Maybe?"

"I know. It has to be Faust," Eden suggested.

"His match has to be out there. I think there's a whole other side of Faust we haven't seen," Harper suggested.

"Are you fucking kidding me?" roared through the door of the conference room. Faust's voice seemed to carry.

"She's going to have to be someone as tough as he is," Remi guessed.

"Or his complete opposite," Elizabeth guessed. "Who would have matched each of us with our Daddies?"

They all sat quietly thinking about that perplexing question for a few seconds.

Remi shrugged. "It doesn't matter what they're like. I'm looking forward to meeting them."

"Me, too," Carlee agreed, and the others nodded their heads.

"Think we can talk them into story time tonight?" Eden asked.

"Bear said he has a book for Talon to read," Ivy shared.

"Oh, no. This might be dangerous," Elizabeth said with a laugh. "Look. The meeting's over. Ink was made a member. That makes me happy."

A few minutes later, Bear steered Talon over to the Littles. "Talon volunteered to read tonight. I have a new book for him. Go ahead and get settled, Talon. I'll grab it."

"What does he have planned for me?" Talon asked.

"We don't know," Remi admitted. "Thanks for reading to us."

"Of course."

"Here you go, Talon." Bear handed him a book wrapped in a brown bag.

Opening it slowly, Talon peeked in and began laughing. "I'm going to get you for this, Bear. Just expect it."

Talon turned the book around to show everyone the cover. *Mr. Fancy Pants Wins the Prize.* The illustration featured a man in psychedelic bell bottom pants poised with one hand up in the air.

"Oh, this is going to be good," Elizabeth said, settling back against a cushion. She loved her Daddy's dance moves.

AUTHOR'S NOTE

Get ready for the next story in the Shadowridge Guardians MC series coming soon!

Shadowridge Guardians MC

Steele
Kade
Atlas
Doc
Gabriel
Talon
Bear
Faust
Storm

Combining the sizzling talents of bestselling authors Pepper North, Kate Oliver, and Becca Jameson, the Shadowridge Guardians are guaranteed to give you a thrill and leave you dreaming of your own throbbing motorcycle joyride.

Are you daring enough to ride with a club of rough, growly, commanding men? The protective Daddies of the Shadowridge Guardians Motorcycle Club will stop at nothing to ensure the safety and protection of everything that belongs to them: their Littles, their club, and their town. Throw in some sassy, naughty, mischievous women who won't hesitate to serve their fair share of attitude even in the face of looming danger, and this brand new MC Romance series is ready to ignite!

ALSO BY PEPPER NORTH

Shadowridge Guardians

Combining the sizzling talents of bestselling authors Pepper North, Kate Oliver, and Becca Jameson, the Shadowridge Guardians are guaranteed to give you a thrill and leave you dreaming of your own throbbing motorcycle joyride.

Are you daring enough to ride with a club of rough, growly, commanding men? The protective Daddies of the Shadowridge Guardians Motorcycle Club will stop at nothing to ensure the safety and protection of everything that belongs to them: their Littles, their club, and their town. Throw in some sassy, naughty, mischievous women who won't hesitate to serve their fair share of attitude even in the face of looming danger, and this brand new MC Romance series is ready to ignite!

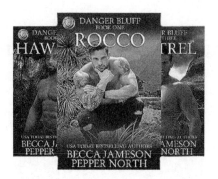

Danger Bluff

Welcome to Danger Bluff where a mysterious billionaire brings together a hand-selected team of men at an abandoned resort in New Zealand. They each owe him a marker. And they all have something in common– a dominant shared code to nurture and protect. They will repay their debts one by one, finding love along the way.

Available on Amazon

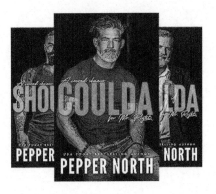

A Second Chance For Mr. Right

For some, there is a second chance at having Mr. Right. Coulda, Shoulda, Woulda explores a world of connections that can't exist... until they do. Forbidden love abounds when these Daddy Doms refuse to live with regret and claim the women who own their hearts.

Available on Amazon

Little Cakes

Welcome to Little Cakes, the bakery that plays Daddy matchmaker! Little Cakes is a sweet and satisfying series, but dare to taste only if you like delicious Daddies, luscious Littles, and guaranteed happily-ever-afters.

Available on Amazon

Dr. Richards' Littles®

A beloved age play series that features Littles who find their forever Daddies and Mommies. Dr. Richards guides and supports their efforts to keep their Littles happy and healthy.

Available on Amazon

Dr. Richards' Littles®

is a registered trademark of

With A Wink Publishing, LLC.

SANCTUM

Pepper North introduces you to an age play community that is isolated from the surrounding world. Here Littles can be Little, and Daddies can care for their Littles and keep them protected from the outside world.

Available on Amazon

Soldier Daddies

What private mission are these elite soldiers undertaking? They're all searching fShadowridge Guardians MCgirl.

Available on Amazon

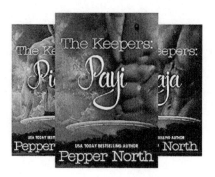

The Keepers

This series from Pepper North is a twist on contemporary age play romances. Here are the stories of humans cared for by specially selected Keepers of an alien race. These are science fiction novels that age play readers will love!

Available on Amazon

The Magic of Twelve

The Magic of Twelve features the stories of twelve women transported on their 22nd birthday to a new life as the droblin (cherished Little one) of a Sorcerer of Bairn. These magic wielders have waited a long time to take complete care of their droblin's needs. They will protect their precious one to their last drop of magic from a growing menace. Each novel is a complete story.

Available on Amazon

ABOUT THE AUTHOR

Ever just gone for it? That's what *USA Today* Bestselling Author Pepper North did in 2017 when she posted a book for sale on Amazon without telling anyone. Thanks to her amazing fans, the support of the writing community, Mr. North, and a killer schedule, she has now written more than 80 books!

Enjoy contemporary, paranormal, dark, and erotic romances that are both sweet and steamy? Pepper will convert you into one of her loyal readers. What's coming in the future? A Daddypalooza!

Sign up for Pepper North's newsletter

Like Pepper North on Facebook

Join Pepper's Readers' Group for insider information and giveaways!

Follow Pepper everywhere!
Amazon Author Page
BookBub
FaceBook
GoodReads
Instagram
TikToc
Twitter
YouTube
Visit Pepper's website for a current checklist of books!

Don't miss future sweet and steamy Daddy stories by Pepper North? Subscribe to my newsletter!

Printed in Great Britain
by Amazon